Next Time
Erin O'Reilly

Next Time

Erin O'Reilly

Affinity
eBook Press
NZ
2016

Next Time
© 2017 by Erin O'Reilly

Affinity E-Book Press NZ LTD
Canterbury, New Zealand

1st Edition

ISBN: 978-0-947528-18-8

All rights reserved.

Editor: CK King
Proof Editor: Alexis Smith
Cover Design: Irish Dragon Designs

Acknowledgments

Back in 2004, I started writing this story and for some reason never finished it. Finding the story again after twelve years, I found myself once again intrigued by the characters and their story and have finished their tale.

I cannot say enough thanks for the support and generosity of time that Julie, my friend and mentor, gave to me and this story. Without her insight and gentle encouragement *Next Time* would still be unfinished. Thank you, my friend.

Thanks also goes out to Nancy who did the last beta edit of the story. I can always count on her to ferret out the places where I didn't make sense or needed to explain further. You're the best!

It takes a village to publish a book and all the wonderful women at Affinity do a fantastic job of taking a raw manuscript and transforming it into a book. Thank you, CK, for your excellence in line editing and with the brilliant addition to the back of the book. Alexis, thank you for the proof editing. Lisa, thanks for giving the story one final read. Alice, I am always grateful for all you do getting my book ready for publication. I am indebted to you all.

Dedication

For Alice

Table of Contents

Also by Erin O'Reilly

Ready for Love
Return to Me
If I Were a Boy
Through the Darkness
Deception
Fearless
'55 Ford
Fractured
Specter of Fear
That Kiss
Revelations
Wolf at the Door
Sandcastles

Writing with JM Dragon

Take Me As I Am
Against All Odds
Earthbound
Quest for Love
New Beginnings
Atonement

When Hell Meets Heaven Series
Echoes of the Past
Paradox of Love
Then End Game

Chapter One

Carol—Lost

The sound of running water wakes me from a blissful sleep. Opening my eyes, I stare at the white swirled ceiling in room three-twenty-five in the Hotel Monaco in Washington DC. My body is naked, and I am sure I still feel kisses lingering everywhere as the taste and smell of Jac fills my senses. Never in my wildest imaginations could I believe anything or anyone could move me to such a passionate encounter. Yet, here I am, pulling back the soft, white sheet, letting my bare feet touch the richly carpeted floor, walking toward the bathroom, and opening the door. I can't help myself. I want—no need—to feel her luscious body next to mine again.

How is this possible? How did I get to this place? Just ten days ago, I thought my life was complete. I was wrong.

✝

It was just like any other Wednesday, or so I thought. I lean back in my chair, trying to block out the images of the abuse Connie Hanson has just shared with me.

Twenty-six years ago, I began working at the health department as a social worker, and I'm still here. From my earliest recollections, my father always told me to have a

1

contingency plan along with a backup. I think that philosophy is what helps me survive my profession. Too many of my associates have become another statistic of a job with a very high burnout rate. How can someone survive the heartache and ugliness as a social worker without a backup plan? I never have taken on a case that surprises me and that is my redeeming quality. Now, I am the supervisor of a group of devoted social workers and trying to impart my father's philosophy on them.

I am happily married to Mike who works for a large corporation that specializes in making light bulbs—I smile at the joke we share about the company where he works. College sweethearts, we married right after graduation and settled down in a little 'shuttered house with a white picket fence.' A year later our son, MJ, Mike Junior, came into the world and my role of wife and mother began in earnest. Two years later, when Kathleen was born, we became the perfect all-American family. I began working for the county health department when Kathleen began preschool and have been here ever since.

The kids are all grown up now, and Mike and I are once again getting to know each other. Mike Junior is a computer engineer who travels around the world installing and troubleshooting multimillion dollar computerized machines for hospital operating rooms. He and his wife Janet and their two children live an hour away. Yep, I am a grandmother...imagine that. Our daughter, Kathleen, is a psychologist living in LA with her husband, Richard Michelson.

I am thinking *life is good* on the day I meet Jac.

†

As with most of the working Wednesdays for the past twenty years, I am looking forward to having lunch with my friend, Evelyn Delarosa. After the grim pictures and details of the child abuse case and the ensuing meeting with the police, I am ready for a nice, relaxing hour away. The phone rings and when I hear Evelyn's voice my heart sinks.

"Hey, we need to change the plans—"

"You're not canceling on me are you? After the day I've had, I don't think I can handle not going to lunch with you."

Evelyn's deep resonating laugh lets me know we're still on. "Like I'd cancel on you today…it's your turn to pay." Clearing her throat, she continues, "I do have a bit of a problem though."

"A bit of a problem? Yeah right, you never have a bit of anything. What's up?" As long as I've known her, Evelyn faces life with gusto at a hundred miles an hour.

"We have visitors from DC, and I need to bring one of them along with me."

I smile. Evelyn never does anything because she has to. I know there is more to the story. "So what's the real reason?"

"If I don't, this person will have to suffer through lunch with the exec and his staff."

"Oh God, not that, by all means bring him along."

"Her," she corrected. "I'll pay this week."

"Now, Evelyn, you know how confused I get with whose week is whose. It will be my pleasure to pay for everyone's lunch. It's not often I get to rescue someone from the clutches of the county exec. I'll meet the two of you at Vinny's at the usual time."

"Yep, later then. Bye."

†

While walking toward the building, I can see Vinny's is already teeming with patrons. Once I arrive at the door, I excuse myself past the crowd of people and enter the restaurant. Once again, I meet another group of waiting diners in a small alcove. The smell of tomatoes, basil, and garlic assaults my nostrils, and my mouth waters.

I smile when I see Gio waving me toward him. Giovanni and Anthony Vincent own the small Italian restaurant that Evelyn and I have frequented most Wednesdays ever since they opened ten years earlier. In fact, I recall that we were some of their first customers, and Giovanni and Anthony have never forgotten us. No matter how crowded they are, a decent table is always available for us.

"Hello, Lady, where is your friend today?" Gio asks. "I have a table ready for you." He leads me to a table in a secluded corner. I can hear the other patrons who were waiting begin protesting loudly, to which Gio mumbles something that sounds like Italian cursing.

"She will be along, Gio. We have a third today, will that be a problem?"

"Of course not," he says before telling the busboy, "there will be three here."

The young man then brings another place setting to the table as Gio pulls out my chair. "Thank you."

"My pleasure, Lady. I will send your friends back when they get here."

I look around at the familiar atmosphere and, for the first time this day, I feel contentment as my shoulders begin to relax. In the distance, I see Evelyn's short, greying head of hair bobbing in my direction.

Evelyn has always been the best dressed person I know and today is no exception. She has on a long dress with matching shoes and, of course, her jewelry is coordinated too. We first met when we both started working at the health department on the same day. She was the personal assistant to the Director of Health, while I was just beginning as a social worker. We had gone through orientation and shared a table at lunch and have gravitated toward each other ever since. I remember when I first saw her; she reminded me of Billie Jean King in stature and looks. Much to my surprise, I found out that she was an avid tennis player and still is all these years later.

An instant smile crosses my friend's face when she sees me waving her over to the table.

"Where's your DC visitor?"

"Right behind me, I hope. She and Gio were having a conversation in Italian, and he said he would show her to the table when they were through." She smiles and winks at me. "She's a looker and you know how Gio likes the women."

Looking up, I see the owner heading toward us, talking animatedly to the most stunning woman I've ever seen. I'm sure I look like an idiot sitting here with my mouth open until Evelyn asks, "Is something wrong?"

I quickly regain my composure and say, "No, I think your visitor is on her way." I nod in the direction of the two people who are about to arrive at the table.

"Here you are," Gio says, as he pulls out a chair for the woman.

For someone who prides herself on never being surprised, the disarming smile and fond pat on the hand that the woman gives Gio, does exactly that. "*Grazie.*" That one word sends a shiver down my spine. I'm not sure if it is the sound of her voice or the way the word seems effortlessly to run off her tongue that catches my attention. The sense of dèjà vu is so overwhelming that I am certain I have heard that voice before.

"Carol, this is Jacqueline Reinhart, who is visiting us from the Department of Health and Human Services." Even though my friend is trying to act as though it's no big deal, I can tell the woman's importance impresses her.

"Nice to meet you, Jacqueline," I direct toward the woman whose blue eyes are fixed on me.

She holds out her hand and I take it, marveling at the softness and power. The touch elicits a pleasurable feeling spreading throughout my body and, in that instant, I know I want more.

"Nice to meet you too, Carol. Please call me Jac."

Reluctantly, I let go of her hand. "Any special reason for your visit to our fair city, um…Jac?"

The same disarming smile she'd given Gio focuses on me. "I am getting together a team to see if we can streamline any of the social services we offer, both nationally and locally." She turns toward Evelyn. "I am particularly impressed by the solid record of service this city is providing its citizens."

Obviously, Evelyn was under the woman's spell too, for I see her blushing for the first time in all the years I've known her. Evelyn acts as the liaison between the health department and the county executive's office. It is because of the implementation of her plans that the department runs so smoothly.

"Jac has asked for a representative from our department to join her in DC next week. She'd like us to lend some of the ideas we incorporate to a national program modeled after ours and several other cities." She reaches for her beeper that is lying on the table vibrating. "Sorry, I need to see what this is about." She gets up from the table and moves away.

The truth is that I am glad for the chance to be one on one with Jac. How can I describe this woman? For that matter, how can a person objectively describe anyone who assaults their mind and body? She is taller than my five foot six inches. I guess she is probably around five eight or nine. Her shoulder length wavy black hair is lustrous. The navy blue suit she is wearing accentuates her eyes, making them bluer. They don't seem to be a true blue, and I wonder if they change when she wears different colors.

Her body is soft yet firm—if that contradiction in terms is at all possible. I feel sure that at one point in her life it was what one would consider a 'killer body.' Now, with time, it has gone a bit soft but still tempts quite a few, I am certain. I remember her walking toward me and how I noticed her long, shapely legs. She is breathtaking. I am wondering where that thought comes from when Evelyn returns to the table.

"Sorry, I must get back to the office. There seems to be a bit of an emergency that cannot be handled without me." She narrows her eyes then shakes her head. "Jac, I will leave you in Carol's capable hands until the meeting at two in the third floor conference room." Evelyn gives us what I think is a beleaguered smile as she gets ready to leave. "You," she says looking at me, "I will see later."

As I watch my friend walk away, I find myself glad she's going. How odd—I want this magnificent woman all to myself. I can feel my cheeks get hot with the thought and quickly lift the menu up over my face.

"They have a very good antipasto salad, if you are interested in something along that line. Also, they make a wonderful chicken-parm sandwich if you feel like being decadent." I peer over the menu and see what look like amused blue eyes. "Is something funny?"

Her hearty, deep laugh makes my skin tingle. "Chocolate is decadent. I've never heard anyone refer to anything chicken as decadent."

I can feel my face get hot with a blush, and I wish the table would engulf me.

Once again, that disarming smile brightens her face. "That's cute."

"Cute? What's cute?" *Please let a tornado swoop down and get me out of here,* is the prayer I send up to the weather gods.

"You ladies ready to order?" says the harried voice of our waiter.

I feel my body relax with the words. "Yes, I'll have a grilled chicken salad and a diet soda."

"And what will you have?" the waiter asks, looking at Jac.

A wry smile crosses her lips. "I have it on good authority that your chicken parmesan sandwich is decadent."

"Oh, yes, ma'am, it's the best in town."

Jac closes her menu and hands it to the waiter. "Then that's what I shall have, along with a cup of coffee."

"Good choice," I say with a laugh. "I think a really good hamburger can also be decadent."

Jac laughs again. "I'll keep that in mind."

When Evelyn left, Jac never moved so she is still sitting next to me, and I see her eyes fixing on me. They seem to be searching and dissecting my inner being. Finally, when the waiter brings our drinks, she looks away then speaks.

"I'm really glad that circumstances allowed us to have lunch together, Carol," she says softly. "I've been studying social services departments all over the country for the past three months. The one here is, by far, the most outstanding for productivity and retention. I was especially impressed with your department. How have you managed to have such a high case-load ratio and such a low dropout rate of workers?" Her brow furrows. "Evelyn tells me that it was your revamping of the system that made all the difference."

Again, I blush. "Evelyn is a good friend, but her claims are a bit over zealous. It was a joint effort on everyone's part."

"Would you mind sharing?"

"Not at all. It is very simple really. We figured out a man wrote the job descriptions."

Jac's face seems to brighten in surprise. "A man is responsible for poor social service practices? Just how did you figure that one out?"

It is obvious to me, but glancing at her ring finger and seeing no ring, I figure she might not understand. "Whoever wrote the job descriptions obviously has never done any hands-on social services work. Many job descriptions are written with unrealistic standards. Some are even substandard. I have often suspected that somewhere out there is a template of a blanket job description for all jobs. Besides, we all know men always have to go around the barn six times before going in the front door."

She laughs. "You're probably right on that one. So, tell me, what changes did you make?"

Now it is my turn to look deep into her eyes, because I want to know if she really is interested. Finding no discernable deception, I open my purse and take out a pen and a small notebook. I am now in my comfort zone and zealously answer, "Let me draw you a diagram of how we saw the problems and the remedies we came up with to correct them."

Soon, our heads are together as I show her our plan while answering her thoughtful and knowledgeable questions. Our food arrives and goes untouched, our discussion occupying our mouths. Gio arrives at our table, startling us out of our intense dialogue.

"Lady, there is a phone call for you." He holds out a phone.

"For me?" I ask.

"No." He gives Jac the phone.

"Jacqueline Reinhart." She sounds business-like in her tone and manner yet smiles when she looks in my direction. "I had no idea it was that late. I'll be there in ten minutes." Ending the call, she looks at me apologetically. "Do you realize it's after two?"

I'm sure my eyes show my surprise. "Wow, I had no idea. We never touched our food."

She reaches over and hesitantly touches my hand. "I enjoyed every minute." Her hesitation seems uncharacteristic. "Do you think we could get together for dinner and continue our discussion and maybe even eat our food?" Jac looks at our untouched food and grins.

Something is happening to me that I can't put into words. The thought of Jac leaving is just as overwhelming as the idea of seeing her again. "Why don't you come to my house and have dinner with my husband and me?"

She looks away. "No, I can't do that." After putting a twenty on the table before getting up, she says, "Perhaps another time then."

This turn of events dumbfounds me, so I quickly gather up my belongings and start after her. "Jac, wait up, I'm going the same way." She turns and in that one moment, I am lost, truly lost.

"Come on then, I'm late."

"Not to worry, I know a shortcut." For some reason unknown to me, I take her hand and squeeze it. "So where are you taking me for dinner tonight?"

There is that disarming smile again. "Shortcuts are good, but sometimes it is the long patient way that is the most rewarding. As for dinner, it will be someplace special."

Her voice seems laced with such sensuality that I am finding it hard to speak. "This way," I say, tugging on her

10

arm and pointing toward a side street. "This will put us directly in front of the building."

†

While we are standing in a crowded elevator, she leans over and whispers, "I'll stop by your office when the meeting is over and we can discuss dinner."

I turn, look at her, and try to shake the feeling that we have met before. How can that be—we just met two hours ago. I watch as she exits the elevator, and I am not sure my knees will continue to support me. Once the doors close and she is gone, I lean against the cold metal wall wondering what is going on with me.

My mind is in a whirl with thoughts and visions of Jac, while I walk to and enter my office. I suddenly remember where I had seen her before and walk quickly to the stack of journals waiting for me to read. "I know it is here somewhere. Damn, which month was it? At last." I pull out an issue. There on the front cover is a smiling Dr. Jacqueline Reinhart. "A Fresh Approach to Health Care Issues" is in bold letters under her name. Sitting at my desk, I begin to read the article when the phone rings. My stomach does a roll in anticipation of hearing Jac's voice. No such luck. It is back to the real world, although I'm not sure I'll be able to concentrate with Jac floating around in my head.

I check my watch once more and it is indeed after five and so far no Jac. My stomach has a sinking feeling as I fight with myself about what to do. Earlier at four I called Evelyn's office only to find that she had left for the day. Distracting thoughts invade my mind. Evelyn's leaving for the day makes it obvious that the meeting is over. Maybe Jac couldn't find my office. I reject the thought as I come to the realization that she played me. She only wanted my ideas and, once she had them, I was history. What an idiot I am. *Shit I know better, yet I fell for her line.*

"Damn." I get my things together and head out the door for home.

Once home, I rush around making dinner since waiting for Jac had made me late. I hear the door open and watch as Mike walks into the kitchen before he kisses my cheek. For a moment, the sting of the afternoon dissolves until Jac's words creep into my mind once again. *I'll stop by your office when the meeting is over and we can discuss dinner.* Fortunately, I am chopping onions so the tears in my eyes go unquestioned.

"Something smells good," Mike says, as he sneaks a taste of a tomato. "I thought you weren't going to be here."

"Hey, keep out of that. It's all I have and it's for dinner. Plans changed, so here I am making your meal." I know my tone is harsh and I am instantly apologetic. "I'm sorry. It has been a bad day and I'm running late."

"No problem," he says, as he begins sorting through the mail. "Want to talk about it?"

"Not right now. Maybe later."

I turn and look at Mike as he leaves the kitchen and find myself mystified again by my reaction toward Jac. From the moment I saw her, I had the oddest feeling that we were somehow connected. It was as though she were a long-forgotten memory that was screaming for release. "That wasn't me at lunch. It was someone else," I mumble. *That wasn't me who found herself turned on by the woman. No way.* Yet, just thinking about Jacqueline Reinhart sends all my senses tingling.

I let my defenses down and she used me. "Damn." Tears stream down my cheeks, and I'm not sure I can stop them. "Shit." Two hours with her and I'm shattered. I try to pull myself together by breathing deeply. I need to finish making dinner, but another wave of sadness engulfs my mind.

Mike returns from changing his clothes and, at last, I'm able to carry on in some other way than as if someone died. He sets the table and I put the final additions on the hastily made dinner. I think of the salad I left on the table at lunch and realize I haven't eaten since breakfast. All of a sudden, I am ravenous and, after we sit down, I begin to inhale my dinner. Half-heartedly, I listen to Mike rattle on about his day and I realize this is what is real. This is what my life is about, and there is no room for anyone else.

Standing in the bathroom and looking at myself in the mirror, I wonder how I've let myself get to this point. Somehow, I let a woman named Jac enchant me in such a way that I began thinking about her sexually. That's not who I am, yet here I am looking at myself wondering who it is I'm seeing. Is this the true me? Have I suppressed such feelings all my life? What is it about the woman that I found so appealing that I was willing to…what? I don't know and that is the most disturbing thought I have.

I can't remember ever feeling so emotionally drained, and I crawl under the covers of my bed finding some solace in the feeling of protection they give me. Tomorrow, I will face her with my armor in place. I won't let her affect me like she did again.

I wake in the middle of the night, dreaming about Jac. A vision of her in my arms kissing me and caressing my body creeps into my mind and I want more.

Once again, I am lost.

Chapter Two

The next morning, I drag myself into my office glad that no one knows what a fool I made out of myself over Jac. The sting of her rejection still smarts. I don't understand why I reacted that way, for she never once acted as if she was interested in me in any way other than professionally. Yet, I feel drawn to her and that has never happened to me before. Sure, I had my flirtations and even a kiss or two with someone other than my husband, but nothing compares to the undeniably intense feelings I had—still have—for Jac.

I sit down in my chair shaking my head while I look over my schedule for the day. Most days I'm anxious to get on with what lies ahead, but the enthusiasm I usually feel doesn't exist this morning. Nonetheless, I soldier on and pick up the phone to check my voice mail.

"You have six new messages," the generic woman's voice tells me. "First message…" I listen, taking notes so I can respond later. I hear a voice say, "Carol, this is Jacqueline Reinhart. I'm so sorry I didn't get back to you before you left. I was stuck with the county executive until six thirty, and by the time I finally got to your office, you had left and I didn't want to disturb you at home. Can I make it up to you by taking you to lunch today? I promise we will get to eat it this time. Please, call me."

My heart skips a beat and my body is on fire, as I listen to her message again before realizing that I have no idea how to get in touch with her. "Shit. Now what do I do?" My mind is in a freefall as I try to figure out how to get in touch with Jac. "Evelyn, I can call Evelyn." The only problem—how do I ask for the phone number of a woman that I have no reason to call? "Damn it all to hell. This needs a personal touch." I look at my watch. It's still early, and I don't think Evelyn is in her office yet.

After an hour of anxious waiting, I head for Evelyn's office, trying to devise a plan for obtaining Jac's number. Nothing I can think of seems plausible, so I will have to wing it.

†

I walk into Evelyn's office and when she looks up she smiles. "Hey, what brings you to my neck of the woods?" she asks cautiously. "Someone hasn't let the cat out of the bag have they?"

Confused by what she says, I ask, "Let the cat out of what bag? Evelyn, you know I'm allergic. What in the world are you talking about?"

I can see a look of pure joy on my friend's face. "Close the door please and take a seat."

I do as she asks and sit in the indicated chair. "What's going on?"

Evelyn comes around her desk and sits down next to me before patting my arm. "Something wonderful has happened, Carol." Her smile broadens. "They want you to be part of the symposium on reforming the welfare system in

15

DC next week. Jacqueline Reinhart asked for you personally."

I know I'm sitting there with my mouth wide open, but
I don't know what to say. "I...I can't believe it. Why? Why
me?" I suddenly wonder why Jac would ask for me.
"Shouldn't you be the one to go?"

"We spent all afternoon together, then with the exec
until after six. The only thing that was agreed upon from the
beginning was that you would be our representative at the
symposium."

"You mean everyone thought that? You didn't have to
convince them?"

"Nope. No convincing needed. They came from DC
with your name on their lips, my friend." I feel Evelyn's arm
go around my shoulders and she hugs me close.

To say I am in shock is an understatement. "Wow, this
is unbelievable,"

"You deserve this, Carol. I'm so proud of you."

I'm still trying to digest everything when I hear a
knock on the door.

"Come," Evelyn calls out.

As the door opens, I turn to see Jacqueline Reinhart entering Evelyn's office and I quickly try to avert my eyes. The
last thing I want to do is be caught staring at the woman who
has consumed my thoughts since I met her. I push myself up
from my seat and start toward the door. "I'll leave you both
to your work."

As I pass her by, Jac gently takes hold of my arm and
looks at me but speaks to Evelyn. "Did you tell her, Evelyn?"
she asks.

"Of course." Evelyn has a pleased look on her face.

"And, will you be joining me in DC, Carol?"

"Of course she will," Evelyn blurts out. "Why
wouldn't she? This is the chance of a lifetime for her."

Jac seems to be studying my face. "I only want her to be there if that's what she wants." Her words are close to a whisper, and I detect a slight tremor to her voice before she releases my arm. The warmth of her touch lingers. "It will be counterproductive if she goes only because it is a good career move." Her eyes focus on Evelyn. "This symposium is too important to have the attendees just be there as bodies. I need people who will give credible input to help find solutions."

Both of the women look in my direction, and I feel taken aback by the intensity of the moment. While looking directly at Jac I say, "I want to be there and learn as well as contribute."

Jac's face beams with a brilliant smile. "Terrific."

"I'll go now." I reach for the door.

"Carol, when I'm done here, is it okay if I come by your office? We need to go over the itinerary."

The need to turn and look at Jac once again is so over-whelming that I want to savor every moment and slowly turn back toward her. "I should be there all morning." Afraid that either Evelyn or Jac would somehow detect my racing heart, I quickly turn away and leave.

I walk briskly back to my office with my head swirl-ing. The sounds, the touches, and the sight of Jac are invad-ing all my senses. Once again, I am lost.

†

Back in the safety of my office, I pick up the phone and I dial Mike's number. "Hi, guess what? I've been invited to a symposium next week in DC."

"Next week? For what?" I can tell my words have con-fused him. He is often like that when I say things he isn't prepared to hear.

17

"They are assembling a group of social workers to brainstorm on how to reform the welfare system." I then go into detail about the meeting and how prestigious this is.

"Congratulations, sweetheart." I can hear the pride in his voice. "What do you say I take my favorite girl out to dinner tonight and celebrate?"

"I was hoping you would say that." Bess Mitchell, another social worker, comes to my door and I motion for her to come in. "Mike, I need to go. I'll see you later, bye."

I shake my head, knowing I will need to concentrate on the case Bess wants to consult about, but Jac keeps invading my thoughts. I try to figure out what's going on with me and realize that I am acting like some lovesick school kid. Every thought of Jac is beginning to set off pleasurable feelings in my body, and I find that alarming but, at the same time, I'm sure if I die on the spot it will be with a smile. She hasn't given me any indication that she feels the way I do, but that really doesn't matter. I would never act upon these emotions. I just can't—I don't think it is in my nature. Mentally I shrug. *Is it?*

I smile at Bess and hold up a finger. "Give me a minute." I open a folder lying on my desk and scan it to familiarize myself with Bess' current case. Reading the report of neglected and helpless children, I wonder if the symposium next week will find a way to stop the downward spiral of some families.

"What are you proposing, Bess?"

"I think we need to have the children put into foster care until the parents can get counseling. To date, they have ignored all directives and have failed to meet even the minimum requirements."

"I agree. Go ahead and call child protective services and get those kids out of there today."

"Will do."

I watch as Bess leaves and can see why the dropout rate is so high among social workers—it is the depressing workload. I think the success of this department is partly because we use a team approach to each case. To a degree, this alleviates the tendency for one person to get so embroiled in a case that they lose track of their job and themselves.

I feel eyes upon me and look up to see Jac standing in the doorway. I smile, but for the life of me, I can't think of anything to say. She overwhelms me with feelings I never expected, and I'm finding that very disconcerting. Deep down, I know that we've met somewhere, but I just cannot seem to figure out where that was.

A smiling Jac moves farther into my office. "Did you get my message I left earlier about having lunch with me?" she asks.

So much has happened since my arrival this morning that my mind isn't processing her words. Finally finding my voice, I say, "Yes. Yes, I did. Are we still on?"

"Absolutely." She moves in even closer, and I wonder if I will ever breathe again. "Why don't we go now and then we can spend the afternoon discussing next week." She hesitates. "If that's okay with you?"

I turn my eyes away from her gaze for fear of mine betraying me. "Sounds good to me. Before we go, I'll need to get the names of several hotels from you so I can make reservations." I am trying to sound casual in her presence, but I know I'm failing miserably.

"No need. It's already taken care of. You have a room at the Hotel Monaco on Capitol Hill." Her voice sounds authoritative, but her smile is beguiling.

I really don't know what to say, for this wasn't what I'd expected. "Ah, Jac, I know that hotel. My husband and I thought about staying there on a visit to DC once. I know how extravagant it is. I'm sure with the budget cutbacks

19

we've had that the department can't afford for me to stay for five days in a hotel that expensive. I'll need something less pricey."

Her laugh causes me to shiver.

"It is already taken care of by my discretionary fund for the conference." She moves toward the door in a fluid motion, capturing my attention immediately.

"I don't understand. Did you get a really great discount for the symposium? Is that where the meetings are being held?"

"Shall we go?" She winks at me and I feel giddy. "I parked my car in the garage across the street."

"Don't you want me to drive?" I ask, wondering why she didn't answer my questions.

Again, I hear that laugh and my knees go weak.

"Nope, I have made all the plans. After standing you up last night it's the least I can do."

"You were busy with the exec. It's understandable. It really wasn't a problem." I do not want her to know about the tears I shed. Deep down, I know that she would be upset knowing that she made me cry.

As she maneuvers her rented red convertible out of the city, I note that she is a confident driver. "You seem to know where you are going. Did you grow up around here?"

She looks in my direction before looking back at the highway. "Yes, I know where I'm going and no, I didn't grow up around here." She pauses as she comes to a stop sign and puts on the blinker. "I felt so bad when I was delayed last night that I scouted out the perfect place for lunch today. I asked the concierge at the hotel I'm staying at to find the perfect place, but I didn't care for his suggestions. Evelyn finally was able to recommend a place to go.

"Of course, I knew of your invitation to join the group in DC and wanted to take you someplace special. I remembered our conversation over lunch yesterday and wanted to take you where you can get something decadent." Slowing the car, she turns into the restaurant.

I look at the sign. "Burt's Burgers?" Her choice of lunch places astounds me.

"You should see your face." Jac is laughing. "Are you disappointed?"

"No. No, not disappointed. I'm just surprised. This doesn't seem like your type of place." I immediately regret my honesty.

"Just what do you think my type of place is?" Her voice sounds happy, but there is definitely an undertone of hurt too. "I thought that anyone who would describe chicken parmesan as decadent." She shrugged. "If this isn't satisfactory we can go elsewhere. I thought you said you liked hamburgers."

"Oh, no. Burt's is the place to go to around here for the best burgers. I wasn't trying to insult you or object to the choice. I'm just surprised that's all."

Suddenly, Jac's voice takes on a cold tone. "I see. Maybe this wasn't a good idea. I'll take you back to the city." She turns the key to start the engine.

Panic fills me as I try to figure out how to save the mess I've just created. Reaching over, I put my hand over hers poised on the key. "Look, Jac, I think we have a problem with interpretation here. Can we start again? Please?" She looks so defeated that my heart is breaking for her. "If it makes a difference, I love Burt's. It is one of my favorite places 'cause they have the most delicious onion rings and the burgers are perfectly greasy and made to order."

Her face begins to soften as she turns toward me. "You aren't just saying that are you?"

I see a bit of a smile on her face and feel off balance. "No, once you get to know me better, you'll find out that I don't say anything unless I mean it."

I see her lift her eyebrow in what looks like doubt.

"Want me to recite the menu?"

Her eyes drift to my hand still on hers then back to my face. "From what Evelyn told me, this place gets five stars across the board. She said they'd make the burger any way I want. That's a definite plus for me." She shrugs then grins. "I'm not a big fan of raw onions." She pulls the key out of the ignition. "Come on, let's go then."

†

Jac suggests that we not talk about anything work re-lated, and I readily agree. Instead, we begin to get to know each other. She is forty-five which surprises me since I had guessed her to be younger. I find her to be very forthright with a wicked sense of humor. She's unmarried, which astonishes me because she seems like the type that men or women would fall all over. She tells me that she just never found the right person and would rather live alone than with someone who did nothing for her. She avoids using a gender reference, and I speculate that maybe she prefers women. The thought makes me smile inwardly.

Like me, she'd graduated with a degree in sociology and worked briefly for an urban health department. She quickly realized that wasn't for her and went back to school for her masters then her doctorate. She has been working for the Department of Health and Human Services for eleven years, working her way up the ranks. Now the Director of

Social Services, she feels that she is making headway in the revamping of the entire system.

She says, "Of course, bureaucracy being what it is, I will be long retired before they decide to change much. Still, who knows what great things might come out of the meetings next week?"

I am just getting to know Jac. She is so complex, yet I have the feeling that what I see is exactly who she is. She is intense, yet doesn't seem to take herself very seriously; while at the same time I can feel her compassion. You can't have our type of job and not have altruistic feelings, even if tucked away in a secret place. It isn't hard to notice her intense opinions about her job and goals in life.

It is fascinating listening to her talk. I find myself enthralled with the fluctuations of her voice. One minute it is light, then soft and sexy, then amused by the antics of a child sitting near us. I want to know everything about her and when it is time to get back to work, I want to drag my feet and find an excuse not to go.

As we are leaving, I hear a song that catches my attention. I stop so I can hear the words.

"What's the matter?" Jac asks.

"This song is very interesting. I was hoping to get some idea of what the title is."

Jac smiles. "Mystery solved. It is 'Sharp Cutting Wings,' and Lucinda Williams is the singer. She's a bit off the grid but one of my favorite artists. I have the album and can loan it to you when you're in town next week."

"Wow, yes, yes I would love that. She has a very earthy sounding voice. It sounds like a cross between blues and country."

She looks in my direction and smiles. "I'll let you have it when you get there. Do you like country and blues music?" She unlocks the car and we get in.

23

"I like all kinds, really, but jazz and blues are particular favorites. That singer has a very compelling voice and the tune is catchy."

She looks over at me and seems to be trying to grasp something to say before she once again astounds me. "That song goes something like this... "

I listen as she sings the song. Her voice is beautiful, and the words to the song are strangely familiar and haunting—I am lost in them.

As we head back toward the city, my mind is in a jumble recalling every word and nuance that made up our lunch conversation. I conclude that having lunch with Jac was a very pleasant experience.

†

Jac places her briefcase on a small table in my office and takes out several documents. "Carol," she says patting the chair next to her. "Why don't you sit over here so we can go over the itinerary for next week?"

I waste no time in doing as requested and gladly sit next to her. Curious, I ask, "How many will be attending?"

Jac cocks her head. "Good question. Since we agreed not to speak about work at lunch, I was wondering when you would get around to asking me that." A small smile quivers around her mouth. "Actually the group is rather small, six maybe seven." She looks at me. "I can see from your expression that the number surprises you."

I can feel myself beginning to blush, so I take a big gulp from a nearby water glass. "I always thought symposium meant a large number of attendees."

A knock at the door interrupts our conversation. I look up to see a man standing in the doorway with a vase of roses. "May I help you?"

"You Carol. Barngate?' he asks.

"Yes." I get up and go to him.

"These are for you."

The man hands me the vase, and I dig in my pocket for something for a tip. Handing him two bills, I take the roses and inhale a deep breath of the perfumed air they create. I smile as I place the vase on my desk before reading the attached card. *I'm so proud of you. Love, Mike.*

"They're beautiful." Jac's voice startles me.

I turn to Jac and smile. "Thank you. They're from my husband." For some unknown reason, I feel a pang of guilt when I look at her. I nervously return to my seat, shuffle the papers around, and avoid meeting her eyes. "Now where were we?"

"I believe you were asking about the number of attendees."

When I look up, I see she has an amused expression.

"This is a very select group. My purpose in this exercise is to develop a working plan and that can only be done with those that are dedicated to that end." Her eyes pierce me as they seemingly slice open my head and enter my brain. "You have no idea do you?"

"Idea? About what?" I'm confused by the question and at the way she is looking at me. "Am I missing something?"

The disarming smile that I first saw at Vinny's reappears on her face. "You haven't a clue about your reputation nationally," she says with what sounds like surprise in her voice. "You were the first one I thought of when this plan was in its infancy."

"How can that be? If I was that important, why did you wait until the last week to invite me?" It is obvious to me that she is feeding me a line of bull.

Jac, once again, penetrates me with her eyes. "Getting the top people in a field all together at one time for a week is a scheduling nightmare, to say the least." She pauses. "I've been in contact with Ms. Delarosa for several months now. Fortunately for me, the most important attendee has the most flexible schedule." She looks at me again, and I think she can see the doubt in my eyes. "Okay, all BS aside, I thought you knew. It wasn't until I met with Evelyn and the county executive yesterday afternoon that I found out otherwise. When I spoke with them two months ago, they assured me you would be available."

Her eyes divert from mine, and I can see obvious embarrassment on her face.

"I'm sorry."

When she looks back at me, there is sincerity on her face.

Finally, it hits me. *What a fool I've been.* Midlife crisis has snuck up on me, and I didn't even realize it was happening. For the last twenty-four hours, I have let this woman invade my thoughts and yes, my body.

I had some half-baked idea about having a tryst with her. The night before, as sleep eluded me, I'd fantasized that she was lying next to me. I'd tried to imagine what it would feel like to have her arms holding me after we made tender love unable to be satiated until exhaustion overcame us and we had to stop. Even thinking of it now makes my body tingle. I realize that it was only a silly dream that will never happen.

I groan inwardly and laugh at how full of myself I am. Why would she think of me in any way other than professionally? She knows I have a husband and that alone sends out a message of being unavailable. I now realize that she is only interested in what I can bring to her symposium. *As if a woman like Jacqueline Reinhart would be interested romantically in someone like me. Get real.*

"No need to be sorry, Ms. Reinhart. I'll attend your symposium and lend whatever thoughts I can." I can feel my back stiffen, as I stand and move away from the table and the close contact with Jac. I want to run and hide as I feel tears stinging the back of my eyes, and my heart is sobbing. I turn away, struggling to avoid looking at her, not wanting to see the look on her face. I'm afraid of what might be there.

I can hear the confusion in her voice as she begins to speak. "I...I... Good, I am glad you will be joining us." I can hear her moving papers about and the closing of her brief-case. "I'll fax you the itinerary and directions to the hotel."

I hear her walk toward the door and I want to call out to her, but I'm too ashamed of what I just said, so I don't. Once I know she is gone and I allow myself to look at the space she just occupied, my heart skips a beat when she re-appears in the doorway. Our eyes meet and it is then that I see hurt and sadness in hers.

"Have I done something to upset or offend you?" she asks pointedly.

It is my turn to be at a loss for words. Do I tell her the truth? Do I tell her that I have been daydreaming about her? Tell her how my body reacts to the thought of her or being in the same room with her?

"No. No, you haven't done anything, Jac." I can feel my eyes darting around the room, as I try to think of some-thing half way sensible to say. "It isn't you. I am put out with Evelyn, who is supposed to be my friend, for leaving me out of the loop on this."

Her eyes search mine. "Are you sure that's all?"

Afraid if I speak my voice will betray my true feelings, I just nod.

"Good." She smiles. "Will you call me and tell me your flight number so I can pick you up at the airport?"

27

"I can grab a cab." My body is trembling, as I lift my eyes to meet hers.

"Nonsense. BWI is a madhouse, and I don't want you frazzled. So, I'll pick you up at the airport and take you to the hotel. Agreed?" She fixes me with a stare that says she won't take no for an answer.

I can feel her powerful yet sincere gaze pulling me in. "Yes, I agree." She has invaded both my mind and body. I knew the moment she returned to my office and I saw the look on her face that I am powerless to fight any request she makes of me. I will be a willing participant in anything she asks of me.

Anything.

"I'm looking forward to working with you." She raises her arm and looks at her wrist watch. "My flight leaves in two hours, so I need to get going. I still need to pack my bags." She smiles that smile again. "We're okay, aren't we?"

"Yes." I swallow hard trying to keep my voice from betraying me.

The look on her face is glorious. "I'm happy. Don't forget to let me know your arrival time." She waves as she turns and disappears from my sight.

I stare at the doorway, and the feeling of being lost is overwhelming.

Chapter Three

Thursday is a blur to me. With every case I review and every conversation I have, Jac occupies my thoughts. Sitting at my desk, I am reading a report and a memory from long ago pops in for a visit. I remember one hot summer night when I was about eleven or twelve and a friend, Betty something or another, was spending the night. We were lying in my bed, and she was saying something about men and women making love and then she was on top of me and we shared a kiss.

I haven't thought of that since it happened, and now it is as clear as a bright, new morning. I remember how pleasurable the kiss felt. The fact that it was another girl didn't seem to bother me. Thinking back to high school, I can also remember having a huge crush on an older girl named Ethel—everyone called her E. I feel a smile come on my face, as I remember drawing a picture of her. I remember proudly showing it to my friends. I can feel my face heat up as I now wonder what they must have thought of me.

I guess, at the time, I knew nothing about lesbians or their lifestyle. An innocent time when, as a youngster, I did what came naturally without any thought of recrimination. Now, here I am all these years later and the thought of making love with Jac is terrifying, yet exhilarating. I wonder how this can be. Over the years, I have flirted with men, even kissed a few, but never considered going to bed with them. Yet, this woman, Jacqueline Reinhart, who has not made any type of overture in my direction, is constantly on my mind.

The thought of her makes me wet and so turned on that I feel the need to cross my legs constantly. There's no doubt in my mind that if asked, I would go to bed with her in a minute. Is she awakening feelings, thoughts, and desires in me that I have long suppressed? I shrug. *Obviously.*

The ringing of my phone brings me out of my daydreams. "This is Carol," I say.

"Hello, Carol, this is Jacqueline Reinhart."

Her voice sends me reeling, as I feel myself come. Catching my breath, I respond, "Jac, how nice to hear from you. Has there been a change of plans? I faxed you my flight plans this morning. Is there a problem?" I can feel myself rattling on, as I try to cover up just how disconcerting her call is.

Her laugh is like music to my ears. "No, nothing has changed and yes, I received your fax. I just wanted to touch base with you and see what you think about the group as a whole?"

Taken aback by her wanting my opinion on the other attendees, I hesitate. "To be honest with you, I have looked over the list and there are only two names I recognize."

"And, those are?"

"Helen Burstein and I attended three conferences together. She spoke at two of them, and I remember being very impressed with her results and her creative approach in problem solving."

"Yes, that was my take on her also. And the other?"

Her voice sounds serious and sincerely interested in my opinion. But I hesitate, wondering if I should be honest. I scratch my cheek wondering how to say something about Ron Cuthbert without sounding judgmental or harsh. "I would rather not say if that's okay with you." I hear an intake of breath that tells me it is not what she wants to hear. "Guess not." I swallow hard, trying to collect my thoughts before I continue. "There's one name on the list that worked here for a time."

"I am aware of that." Her matter-of-fact voice tells me she wants to know more.

Now what do I do? I know she wants me to tell her my opinion, but how can I do that? "Listen, Dr. Reinhart…Jac, I just don't feel comfortable about this. Obviously, the person must have some good points or you wouldn't have invited him to the symposium. I'm basing my opinion on a person I worked with almost twenty years ago. People change, as I am sure he has."

Jac's laugh is rich. "Very diplomatic," she pronounces, "and yet you managed never to say his name."

I can hear her still chuckling as I start to speak. "Sorry. Have I disappointed you?"

"No, not at all." I can hear her shuffling papers. "Actually…"

I sit patiently waiting for her to continue, sure she is going to grill me about Ron further. She remains silent. "Actually what, Jac?"

I hear a deep intake of breath again before she speaks once more. "I was wondering if when you get here Sunday…well…I have tickets for the symphony that evening."

"Oh, don't worry about picking me up if you have other plans. I can take a taxi," I hastily say.

"No, that is not what I meant. I wanted to know if you would like to go with me—it's no fun going alone." Her voice sounds tentative and halting.

Now, it is my turn to be quiet, while I try to digest what she just said. Is she asking me out on a date? "Jac, I love the symphony and would be happy to go with you." I know I'm gushing but can't help myself.

"That's great." I can hear the smile in her voice. Again, there is a long pause. "Beethoven," she seems to blurt out. "It is an all-Beethoven night."

"Oh, I love his music, especially his 6th symphony." I know I have a big goofy smile on my face and hope no one chooses that moment to visit my office. "Thank you for thinking of me," I say sincerely.

"It was easy to do." I hear what I think is a sigh of relief. "I mean, I'm picking you up and all so it seems you are the perfect one to invite. I mean…"

"I know." That is all I can think of to say, because something deep inside of me understands exactly what she is trying to tell me.

"Yes, I believe you do. See you on Sunday, Carol. Take care."

"I'm looking forward to next week. Thanks. Bye."

"Bye," was all she says before she is gone.

Hanging up the phone, my fingers linger on the receiver as I stare into space. She didn't say the word *date*, but I know that is exactly what she meant. I have a date with Jacqueline Reinhart to go to the symphony with her on Sunday. My heart beats rapidly with the realization of what might happen. At the same time, I feel devastating fear.

†

Our SUV is heading down the highway toward the airport. I look over at Mike and notice his strong features. I remember when I first saw him, I thought he looked so handsome. The years have been kind to him. He is my rock in so many ways. I do love him, even though the honeymoon has long been over.

Turning my head, I look out the window at the other cars all jockeying for lane position as we reach the airport. "You can let me off at the curb," I say. "It's ridiculous to pay for the parking garage."

Mike laughs. "I think I can manage to scrape together the money." He reaches over and takes my hand. "I can't have my best girl carrying her own bags and going off without a kiss."

He is so kind and loving. He always has been. I wish I could say the same for myself. I wonder if there can be too much goodness in a person. Sometimes I feel like Mike's kindness is suffocating me. There is nothing that he won't do for me and, at times, I want to scream "back off." I did that once and the look of hurt and dismay on his face was more than I could handle. The work I do is so intense that I need alone time. When I'm home, he is always there hovering asking "what can I do for you," and I bite my tongue to hold back my retort—"just leave me alone."

"Okay, go ahead and have it your way," I tell him as we enter the short-term parking area.

I've checked my bags and have my ticket, as we get on the escalator. Mike takes my hand and holds it as we walk the long corridor toward the gate. I let go of his hand. "It's a long line, so I'd better get in it." I proceed to the check-in desk.

I return to where Mike is sitting and smile. "If you want to go ahead that will be okay, they should be boarding shortly. I'll call you when I arrive and let you know the room number." I see sadness in his eyes. "You're okay with this aren't you?"

He smiles and hugs me close. "Yep, I'm proud of you, babe." He leans over and kisses me good-bye. "Don't forget to call," he says.

They announce that my flight is boarding. "That's me." Turning toward him, I smile and kiss his cheek. "I won't forget. Wish me luck."

"Luck." He hugs me. "But you won't need it. You're the best."

I laugh. "You're prejudiced."

"Maybe a little bit." He caresses my cheek. "Go get 'em."

I feel conflicted walking toward the tunnel that will lead me to the plane. Part of me is sad to be leaving, while the biggest part is brimming with excitement. Jac's face comes to mind, as I find my seat and wait for the plane to take off.

Chapter Four

The captain's voice brings me out of my daydreaming, as he announces our imminent arrival at BWI. I am frightened, yet excited. I know if Jac makes any kind of move in my direction, I will not discourage her. A part of me wants Jac, yet another part hopes it will never happen. I think of Mike and, for a moment, I feel a twinge of guilt. But what I'm feeling for Jac is so overpowering that she becomes my only focus. All else pales in comparison.

After emerging from the plane, I see Jac standing squarely in front of the people gathered there. She looks so hot that I can feel myself becoming wet with excitement. I wave to her; our eyes meet and hold each other's, as I shorten the distance between us. As we meet, she gives me a beguiling smile before engulfing me in a hug.

"Don't you just love airports?" she asks as she releases me. There's no apology or embarrassment on her part for her greeting. "I have been here for an hour just watching the people. It's fascinating." She weaves her hand under my arm, and we begin to walk toward the baggage area. "You can see all the emotions here. People are joyous, sad, tired, irritated. If it can be felt, people at airports feel it."

"Sounds like you study them often," I say trying to combat the overwhelming urge to take her in my arms and kiss her.

"Oh, I love to people watch. I think it is an integral part of the work I do to understand how the human psyche works." She motions to the baggage carousel. "It looks like they are unloading your plane now. What do your bags look like?"

I stop and stand still until she realizes I am no longer next to her. She turns around with a perplexed look on her face, before she walks back toward me. I am in awe of her, as I study her face trying again to remember her from a long-forgotten place. There is a familiarity there, I know I have seen her turn and look at me exactly like that before. Why can't I remember? "Damn," I whisper squeezing my legs together as she gets closer.

"Is something wrong?" she asks.

I begin laughing. "Jac, I can get my own bags." I hold up my arms. "See they both work."

"Too much, huh?"

"Just a bit."

She laughs.

"There, that green one is mine." I start toward the carousel.

Jac, disregards my protestations and effortlessly whisks my bag off the revolving rack. She is a vision of fluid motion and my heart beats with the happiness of being with her. For once in my life, I am going to let life take me where it will. No plans, no backup, just go with the flow. All else is irrelevant at this moment. For me, there is no one else but Jac. If Jac and I are to be lovers, it will be. If not, then maybe we'll become very good friends. A sense of sadness fills me with the last thought.

"Ready to go?" Jac asks.

Her voice is like music to my ears. "Yes, ready to go with you anywhere you take me." I'm shocked by the boldness of my words. Looking at her, I see her cock her head, and I fear that I said the wrong thing. "Is something the matter?" I ask.

She hesitates as if she is studying me, then smiles. "No. Everything is just as it should be."

Her voice is soft and sensual, or so I think. Hell, I think everything about her is hot and desirable. Suddenly, I have a strong desire to run and hide. What the hell am I doing here thinking these thoughts about another woman? Except for the hug, she has given no indication that she wants me or even thinks of me in that way. *I am acting like a dope.*

"It is, isn't it?"

†

The room is magnificent. Never have I seen such opulence in one hotel room. Every amenity is there right down to a plush robe and a goldfish.

"Jac, this is absolutely fabulous." I can't hide my enthusiasm. "How can your department afford something like this for your attendees? You must have gotten some great discount." I wander about the room running my fingers over the rich wooden surfaces and gawking at the high ceilings.

"This building was once the Tariff Building. It was converted into a hotel and opened not too long ago." She smiles. "There's lots of history in this building and preserving that was one of the stipulations for the remodeling that my family, as a major benefactor, insisted upon." Her voice is so soft that I turn to see if she is really speaking. The look on her face is one of happiness, as she describes the hotel. "Are you pleased with the room?"

"Oh, yes, it's wonderful. What do the others think? I bet they are just as astounded as I am."

A strange look crosses Jac's face before it becomes a brilliant red. There's no doubt about it, she's blushing. "I don't know where the others are staying. They're on their own."

Her eyes avoid mine, and I suddenly realize the implications of those words. "Oh, Jac." I put my hand over my mouth and struggle not to go to her and pull her into a hug. I begin toward her, but she saves me from humiliating myself by taking a step back, increasing the distance between us.

"Listen, I've got to go and get ready for the concert. Would you like to have dinner before?"

"Do we have time?" I look at my watch and realize the symphony doesn't start for several hours. "I would love to have dinner with you, Jac. Would you be my guest?" Yep, I'm asking her out on a date. My fingers are plunged deep in my pockets, crossing that she will say *yes*.

There's that look again, and I melt as I see a smile begin to play around the corners of her mouth. "May I ask you if this is a friendly meal or something else?"

I know I have a goofy look on my face, as I cast my eyes to the ground before pinning her with them. "Oh, it is definitely something else. Would you like that?"

"Yes," she whispers.

My feet are closing the distance between us. "So would I." We are within arm's length. "Will you be my date for dinner tonight, Jac?"

Jac's arms surround me as she pulls me close to her. She whispers in my ear, "I'd love to."

Then her lips are on mine, and I melt into her mouth willingly. The kiss ends and I find myself wanting to feel Jac's lips again; so I lean in for more, but she pulls away.

"I'd better get going while I still can," her voice is playful and relaxed. "Can you be ready in an hour? I'll make the dinner reservations if that's okay with you."

Reluctantly, I take several steps backward creating the space that I desperately need but don't want. "Yes, to both." My heart is thumping so hard in my chest that I am sure she can see its rise and fall.

She moves closer to me and kisses my cheek tenderly. "Thank you," she says softly before turning to leave.

My hand reaches up and touches my cheek and I am lost in her.

✝

I can't take my eyes off her as we eat dinner. Actually, I think I have been secretly watching her ever since we first met. Something about her is familiar; like we've met before. I know it sounds strange, but I know Jac—I know her very well.

"I have this feeling that I know you from somewhere, Jac."

She smiles and reaches across the table to touch my hand. "It was about five years ago in Dallas. That's where I first saw you, at a Social Workers of America conference. You were giving a speech on the ethical and emotional support for battered women." Her fingers slide back and forth across mine. "I had just wandered in there to find an associate and was so enthralled by your thoughts and ideas that I didn't want to leave until you finished so I could speak with you personally."

"I'm usually pretty good with faces, and I don't re-member ever meeting you there or anywhere else until last week."

"You didn't. There were so many people surrounding you that I couldn't even get close." She withdraws her hand as a distant look crosses her face. "I can still feel the pang of disappointment I felt when I watched as you left the audito-rium. You feel now like I felt then. I knew you, Carol. I knew you, but didn't know how."

I watch the emotions cross her face and know that she is speaking the truth. "Well, now that you've met me up close and personal, do you still think you know me?"

"I've always known you." A look of peace and happi-ness fills her face as if she just realized a truth she never knew. "As much as I hate to say this, we really do need to get going."

I slide my chair back and get up. Jac is instantly at my side placing her hand in the small of my back as she guides me toward the exit. If the meal was any indication of what the night is going to be like, it will be heaven.

†

The symphony is more than I could have ever hope for in many ways. Just sitting next to Jac and listening to the *Pastoral* is exhilarating. I've never been a feely-touchy type of person and abhor those who are, but I can't help but touch her often. It's not sexual. It is more of a need to connect with her—to be one with her. It feels right.

We arrive back at the Hotel Monaco and silently ride the elevator up to my floor. I can feel the butterflies in my stomach in anticipation of what will happen next. All night, Jac has been attentive and flirtatious, making me quake with the need of her.

40

While standing at the open door, I motion her inside. "How about a nightcap?" I say in my most seductive voice.

Jac steps inside and I close the door. We are but inches apart, as she moves closer still and takes me in her arms. Our kiss is soft and unhurried, as we seemingly melt into each other. Her mouth explores mine before her tongue runs along my lips and I welcome her in. My response is one of want and need.

She pulls away and smiles as her fingers run through my short blonde hair. I am on fire with desire and move in for another kiss only to have her turn away.

"I need to go."

I don't know what to say. Once the contact I have with her is broken, I ask, "I don't understand. Why?"

"Big day tomorrow and, right now, that has to be my only focus." She once again moves closer to me and lightly kisses my cheek. "There will be a car to take you to the meeting in the morning."

I can only stand there with what I am sure is a startled look on my face. Words stick in my throat, as I watch her open the door before disappearing as it closes.

"What just happened?" I move to the door and touch the handle, battling with myself until I open it. I move out into the corridor and look down the hallway only to see the doors of the elevator closing and taking Jac away.

Back in my room, I am unmoving, stunned, and devastated. The flashing of the message light on the phone finally gets my attention. Numbly, I listen to the message. It's from Mike telling me good night. I hold my hands over my face. The last thing I want at this moment is to hear Mike's voice. What I wanted just walked out the door and no platitudes of "good night" are going to lessen the devastation I feel.

"Oh God," I cry. I remove my clothes, letting them fall to the floor. I ignore the chocolate on the pillow and crawl under the cool soft sheets. My naked body quivers, not only from cold but also from disappointment. Tears, falling from the corners of my eyes land in a puddle on the six-hundred-count pillowcase.

Jac has gone and I am here alone, unfulfilled and completely at a loss as to what to do about it.

Chapter Five

I'm not sure when or if I fell asleep. The only thing I am certain of is the insistent ringing of the phone. My eyes open and I see the clock, seven o'clock, and realize that it's my wake up call. I pick up the receiver and return it to the cradle. I stretch, remembering the night before, and fill with an overwhelming sense of sadness. I automatically throw the covers back and sit up with my legs dangling over the side of the bed. I feel myself sighing as I walk into the bathroom.

"It is going to be a long day and an even longer week."

Just as I finish blow drying my hair, I hear a knock at my door. "Jac." A momentary sense of joy fills me, as I open the door only to see a man with a tray on a cart standing there.

"Your breakfast, ma'am." He rolls my breakfast into the room and places each covered item on a white-linen-covered table. "Please," he gestures toward the chair he has pulled out.

"I didn't order this."

"You are Ms. Barngate in room three-twenty-five, aren't you?"

I nod.

"Then this is for you. Please be seated."

I do as he requests and sit down while the man uncovers the meal. Yogurt, a banana, toast with peanut butter, and a diet Coke. I laugh as I hazily remember telling Jac at one point the night before what I'd had for breakfast.

"Perfect." I look at the waiter in question. "Shouldn't I sign something?"

"It's been taken care of, ma'am," he says, as he begins to leave the room.

"Can you wait a moment so I can tip you?"

"Taken care of," he says, as he closes the door.

I can't help the goofy smile I have on my face, as I pick up the toast and take a bite. This one small gesture makes all the hurt disappear. Truth be told, I don't think I could ever be upset very long by anything Jac does.

✝

Entering the conference room, I see Jac speaking with one of the attendees. It is as though she senses me there, for her eyes immediately lock on mine. There's that smile again, and I feel myself melt into her gaze. Whatever last night was about doesn't matter for I'm here and captivated once again.

"Good, I see we're all here now. Take a seat, please, and we'll get started." Jac speaks and the entire room listens. "I know some of you are acquainted and all have the information I sent you about each other, but I think it would be good for us each to introduce ourselves before we begin. Carol, will you start?"

It is not until I see the quirky smile on the face that has my full attention that I realize she is speaking to me.

"Oh, okay. Hello, I'm Carol Barngate, and I suspect, like all of you, social work is all consuming and..."

†

"Somehow, the past seven hours flew by," I say to Jac after the others have left. "That's a definite sign of a great meeting."

I see her smile. "It did go well, didn't it? I think we have an eclectic group of high thinkers." She nods. "This is going to be a good week."

"Yes it is." I look around, trying to think of a reason to stay. "Do you need any help?" Our hands, reaching for the same paper, touch and I feel my body react.

I can tell she feels it too, for she trembles slightly before she moves her hand. "No, I'll leave the materials for tomorrow."

"Do you have any plans for this evening?" I boldly ask. "Want to have dinner with me?"

Jac's eyes seem sad to me, and I hope it isn't something I did to make her look that way.

"I'm sorry, not tonight. I already have other plans."

I can feel a frown fill my face. "Oh, I see." It is impossible for me to hide my disappointment.

"Look, Carol, please understand that I'd like to have dinner with you tonight instead of what I have to do. It is unfortunate that I have another obligation tonight."

Unable to stop myself, I nod and say, "Okay, I'll see you here tomorrow."

She reaches out and takes my hand. "I'm sorry," she whispers.

"Can you come by the hotel for a nightcap once you're done?" I know I'm groveling, but I'm desperate to keep the connection. When I see the look in her eyes, I know I've gone too far. I've allowed myself to become a sniveling hanger-on.

Jac says, "No, I can't. Not tonight."

I realize that being with Jac tonight, or any night for that matter, isn't going to happen and shrug. "Okay." I turn and walk away puzzling over the conundrum known as Jac.

†

Once I enter my hotel room, I kick off my shoes and turn on the television. I look but don't see the action on the screen. I'm too intent on trying to figure out what's happening with me. I know, by the way Jac looks at me and kisses me that she wants more than a professional relationship. But, she keeps pulling away and that has me wondering why.

I yawn and open the menu for room service. Just as I'm about to lift the receiver, the phone rings and my heart rate speeds up. *Jac.* I pick up the phone. "Hello," I say expectantly and immediately feel a distinct disappointment.

"Oh, hi, Mike."

"Are you all settled?"

"Yes, the room is amazing. I just got in and was going to call you."

"How are you doing?"

"I'm doing fine. Just tired, it's been a long day."

"Have you had dinner yet?"

"Not yet." I sigh. "I was just about to order it when the phone rang. I won't get much since I'm not that hungry."

"Any plans for the evening?"

I laugh. "I don't think I have any energy to do anything. What I really want to do is take a bath and go to bed early."

"You're not over doing it are you?" I can hear the concern in his voice.

"No, I'm not over doing it." I stifle a yawn.

"Take care and get a good night's sleep."

"Okay, I will. Good night, Mike. Bye."

I hang the phone up and realize that Mike's call has grounded me and made me realize what is real. What I've been thinking about Jac is nothing more than a fantasy. I dismiss that as my fingers run across my lips and realize that Jac's kiss wasn't make-believe; it was real and it meant something.

†

It's Tuesday morning and the day begins with a breakfast meeting. I'm surprised when Jac takes the seat next to me.

"Good morning," I look at her. Her face is drawn and that makes my heart go out to her.

"Good morning," she says softly. "Did you sleep well?"

I'm about to answer when Ron Cuthbert sits down on the other side of Jac and begins speaking to her. When I knew the man almost twenty years ago, he was a sleaze and from what I've seen yesterday and today, the description still applies. I listen to their conversation and the polite, succinct way Jac replies. Her voice sounds tired, but there is something else in her tone—sadness. I wonder if that is because of whatever engagement she had the night before.

We divide into two groups and discuss viable ways for revamping parts of the system for the balance of the morning. I covertly watch Jac, as she sits alone in one corner of the room focused on a folder of papers. Occasionally, I catch her looking at me with such intensity that I have to look away.

At noon, we break for lunch and all sit loosely around a table discussing our ideas while munching on the catered lunch fare. When I see Jac come back into the room, I smile and she rewards me with a smile before sitting next to me. She scoots her chair closer to mine and the nearness of her literally takes my breath away and I have to suck in a breath. Her fingers touch my thigh, and I look at her. She flashes that quirky smile, and I feel myself react in pleasure.

I lean in closer and ask, "Are you okay?"

She was about to answer when Ron, with his condescending tone, begins to speak. "Why don't we all go out tonight? I know just the place."

Someone from the other side of the table says, "sounds like a great idea," and soon everyone is buzzing about going out as a group.

"Then it's settled," says Ron. "We'll meet at Madam's Organ, for drinks then dinner."

I look at Jac and see that her expression is neutral. "You don't want to go, do you?" I ask softly.

"I was hoping we could have dinner just you and me."

I don't quite understand the mixed signals she is giving me, but I am helpless to do anything but bask in what she offers me. "I would have liked that too. Perhaps tomorrow night."

Jac smiles. "Perhaps." She stands. "Okay, everyone, it's time to get back to it."

I'm glad when the afternoon session ends and everyone gets up and moves away leaving Jac and me the only ones still standing by the table. "I guess there's no way of getting out of Ron's plans," I say.

Jac smiles at me and shrugs. "It'll be fun. I've been to Madam's and I'm sure you'll like it."

I move closer to her. "I'll take your word for it."

Jac closes the distance between us, reaches out, and touches my hand, "Do you want me to pick you up?"

"That would be wonderful, thanks." I smile at her and wonder if tonight will be the night. "I'll wait in the lobby for you."

"No. I don't want you waiting in the lobby. I'll come to your room."

"How long will it take you to get to the hotel?"

"From here? About twenty minutes."

"Okay. Why don't you give me a call when you are leaving, and I will time it so I'm at the curb when you arrive? That way you won't have to fight the traffic to find a parking spot."

"I could use the valet parking, but that sounds like a better plan to me."

I watch as she collects her things. "I guess I'd best get going so I can be ready to go. What time are we all meeting?"

"Ron said he'd make dinner reservations for seven and that happy hour starts at five." She touches my arm, and I lean into the caress. "Why don't I pick you up at six thirty, unless you want to get there earlier for drinks with everyone else?"

"I'm not really into drinking with everyone. There will probably be enough of that over dinner."

Jac nods. "You're probably right. Will that give you enough time to get ready?"

"Yes, I'll have plenty of time." She removes her hand, and I feel bereft at the loss of contact.

†

Madam's Organ is one of those places you have to experience at least once in your life. The place is outrageous and draws you in with the blues soulfully calling out your name. Some of the walls are hot pink—or is that magenta?—

with neon helping to assault my senses and putting me in a party mood.

Jac and I make our way up the stairs to the 'love lounge' and find the others already seated with drinks in hand.

Ron Cuthbert is immediately out of his chair and at Jac's side. He has been unabashed in his flirting with her, and it looks to me like he is trying, once again, to make a move on her.

"Hey, glad you finally got here. Now, the party can start." He motions to the chair next to his. "There's an empty seat right here, just waiting for you."

"Thanks, Ron, but I think Carol and I will sit over there." She takes my arm and leads me farther down the table. We sit next to each other.

I can see the look on Ron's face, and I can tell that Jac's rejection pisses him off. I've seen that look before from him. For a moment, he just stands there, seemingly embarrassed, until his obnoxious nature rebounds. "Hey, Carol, do you remember back in the old days when we would go to the bar across the street from work? What was the name—"

"The Dirty Robber," I offer.

"Yeah, that's it."

Just then, the waiter arrives, distracting Ron and saving me a walk down memory lane with him.

Throughout dinner, I watch, as the others seem drawn to Jac just as they have been since we all first met. For a moment, I wonder if they too are under her spell. I really can't blame them—she's awesome. I discreetly watch her, as I place my hand on her knee. A small satisfied smile crosses her face, before her hand finds its way to rest on mine. During the day, I found myself drawn to her and being with her in the restaurant is no different. The need I have to connect with her is overwhelming. I'm probably channeling my own feelings, but I think she feels the same way for she leans into me whenever I am near.

The nature of the job makes many of us feel the need for release, and this night at Madam's is no exception. The group gets along very well, as the drinks and food flow. Unfortunately, Ron hasn't forgotten that Jac picked me over him and, once again, rekindles the past.

"Way back when," he starts, "Carol here and I worked together. I think it was the first job for both of us. Right?" He looks at me.

I nod hoping he won't pull out too many old memories.

He takes a long draw of his beer. "Anyway, sometimes, after work we would go to this bar, the Dirty Robber, and relax. Do you remember, Carol?"

I roll my eyes.

"This woman,"—he points to me— "could drink anyone in the place under the table. We devised a game called "you buy" where everyone would cut a deck of cards and the lowest card would have to buy the highest a shot. Damn if she won every single time." His eyes challenge mine. "Can you still do that, Carol? I always wondered if it was a trick, because no one can be that lucky all the time."

The man is a jerk and, although I have matured in the years since I saw him last, I am up to the challenge. "I out did you then and can again, Ron. Do you have a deck of cards?"

It's as though he had hoped this would happen, for he pulls a deck out of his pocket and passes it down the table to Jac. "Care to shuffle? We've got to have this on the up and up."

Jac skillfully shuffles the deck and places it face down on the table before tapping the stack with her index finger. Everyone leans in closer. Ron opens his hand and motions, "Ladies first."

I know I have an 'eat my shit' grin on my face, as I cut the deck and lift my draw up for all to see—a ten of hearts.

Ron sighs and laughs, "Oops, I seem to remember you only drew face cards." He then picks up the very next card and shows the table—a five of clubs.

"Looks like you buy the shot." I know I'm being smug, but he has it coming to him.

Unfortunately, everyone wants to try. Six shots later and I still haven't bought a drink. That is when Jac takes over. "Are you ready to go?" she asks me.

The drive back to the hotel is quiet. I can't help but wonder if tonight Jac and I will find our way to each other again. She pulls her car near the entrance and stops, and I realize her plan is to drop me off.

"Want to come up for a nightcap?" I ask desperate for one moment more.

"No, I'm going to call it a night."

This can't be happening—the hands touching, the tender looks, her constant attention— she can't be leaving. I lean over and kiss her cheek. "Please, come up with me."

For a long moment, she gazes at me. "I make it a rule not to take advantage of someone who has had too much to drink."

Now it's my turn to stare. "I'm not drunk." My tone is harsh and I'm instantly sorry. "I know I had a lot of shots, but I'm fine, really. All the water I drank before neutralized the alcohol. I learned that back in college."

"Was it a trick or did you just get lucky seven times selecting a card?"

I laugh mostly out of relief that she hasn't left yet. "It's a gift."

"A gift, ah huh." She laughs. "I need to get going. We have another long day tomorrow, and I'm not used to these late nights."

I reach over and take her hand. I avoid looking at the eyes. "Please, don't go."

She lifts my hand to her lips and kisses it tenderly. "I have to. I'm sorry."

Savagely, I pull my hand from hers and open the door. I will not let her see me cry. Once I'm out of her car, I slam the door before walking with purpose to the entrance. I am hoping to hear a car door open and her footsteps coming after me—I don't.

Once in my room, I sit poised on the bed for the knock at the door that never comes. "What game is she playing?"

While taking off my jacket, shirt, slacks, and under-wear, tears are streaming down my face. "I am a stupid old woman with fantasies about someone who only wants to play with my emotions. Never again will I allow Jacqueline Rein-hart to hurt me."

My tears flow freely, and I don't know how to repair my breaking heart.

Chapter Six

Wednesday's meeting is the most productive so far. All day, I have watched Jac expertly guide the group. She is amazing with a quick understanding of concepts and thoughtful contemplation of solutions.

Harold Sampson, a balding man in his mid-forties, who is the director of social services of a large midwestern city, is my partner for this part. We are working on the restructuring of divisions and the last section stymies us. No matter where we put the Medicaid division, it seems to cause problems in other areas.

I don't know how to explain the connection I feel with Jac, but I can feel her standing silently behind me. I know she's watching me and taking in everything.

Finally, resting her hand on my shoulder, she leans in between us. I wonder if she feels my body trembling and my heartbeat increasing. If she does, she makes no indication, as she points to one of the groupings on our chart.

"What would happen if you moved this one under the auspices of the director?"

Harold and I look at one another. "That would work, then we can make social services an independent grouping."

Jac's hand is still resting on my shoulder as she straightens back up. When she removes it, the feelings of loss are unbearable. I want to run and hide somewhere, as I feel tears threatening to flow, once again. I remember her rejection of the night before, and I have an overwhelming feeling of distress and sadness.

It is at that moment that our lunch orders arrive, and I am grateful for the opportunity to excuse myself. I walk rapidly down the hallway to the rest room. Once inside the stall, I bolt the door, hoping this will lock out all the emotions raging through my body and mind. I was determined to rid myself of Jac this morning, but I have failed miserably. Her hold on me is stronger than ever. While sitting on the toilet, I bury my face in my hands as the tears begin once again.

I hear the door open and realize I need to pull myself together and stop acting like a love sick puppy. The last thing I need is for someone else from the group to see me crying.

"Carol, are you okay?" Jac's voice asks.

Shit! "Yes," I say weakly, trying to disguise the weepiness of my voice. I wipe the tears away, pull up my pants, and stand. Once I've gotten myself together, I emerge from my hideaway to see Jac standing there.

She's instantly by my side, as I'm washing my hands and dabbing cold water on my eyes. "What's the matter?" she asks softly with her head tilting to look at me.

"Nothing." I take a deep breath, frantically trying to control my shaky emotions.

"Carol," her voice is soft and soothing. "Why have you been crying?"

I clench my teeth, breathe deeply, and straighten my back. "I'm fine." I can tell she's not buying my story, but I push past her and open the door. "Our meals are getting cold.

We should go now." I continue out the door and head back to the conference room.

Five minutes later, Jac returns and joins in as if nothing has happened. I'm grateful, for at this point, I am too fragile for anything emotional.

Finally, the day ends and we all begin to pack up our belongings before heading back to our various hotels. I'm looking forward to a long, hot bath in the claw foot tub and a chance to be alone. Mostly, I want to be away from the influences of Jac and start for the door.

"Carol, could you give me a minute?" Jac asks just as I reach the door.

Damn. I really have no choice but to turn and respond. The others are still in the room, and I certainly don't want them to know my true feelings. I walk back into the middle of the room where Jac is standing.

I look into her beautiful face and see stress and what I think must be exhaustion. My heart goes out to her, but I will not go down that path again. Strictly professional is my new motto. "I think we made great headway today," I say giving her a tight smile.

Her eyes look toward the door and at the last of the participants leaving. "Yes, tomorrow we should be able to have a working model. I'm pleased with the progress."

We stand for a few minutes. "If that's all you wanted, I need to get going. A hot bath is calling my name." I deliberately take a step back, distancing myself from the woman.

"What's your problem?"

"I have no idea what you are talking about. As far as I know, nothing is happening or going on. I came here to attend your symposium, nothing more." I can feel the edge of coldness in my voice, as I take the tone I use with uncooperative clients. I will not let her in ever again.

She tries to move closer to me, but I move away. "Will you have a drink with me? I really think we need to talk."

"There's nothing to say, Dr. Reinhart."

"Please," her voice is soft with an urgency that I haven't heard before.

No matter how hard I try, I cannot stop the tears from flowing. "I can't...it hurts too much."

She attempts to put her arms around me, but I stop her. "Don't."

"What hurts too much, Carol? Please, tell me."

Through my tears I cry, "Your rejection of me."

Except for my occasional sobs, the room is deathly quiet. Unable to look at Jac, I turn away and start for the door to escape from her and my grief.

"It's not rejection," she finally says.

Her words piss me off, and I turn to face her with my anger flaring. "It sure hurts and feels like rejection. Obviously, I misunderstood your actions. It will not happen again. After all, I'm married and that is where my focus is. Now, if you don't mind, I need to go."

I can see the mystified, hurt look on her face, but I will not let her dissuade me. I leave the room. I walk toward the entrance of the building and her face floods my mind.

"No, I will not let her do this to me again," I say shoving the heavy door open and stepping out into the night air. I look around and realize I'll have to walk back to the hotel. My inner voice tells me it's not a great choice. Luckily, I see a taxi approaching and flag it down. It stops and I open the door.

Just as the cab pulls away, I see Jac exit the building. Our eyes lock for an instant and, deep in the recesses of my soul, I know I had finally found what I didn't know I'd lost.

†

It is Thursday and I awaken to the insistent pounding on my door. Groggily, I get out of bed. I spent the night before in the hotel's bar, and the liberal amount of Crown Royal I drank is now pounding inside my brain. "Who is it," I say softly, although my ears and head register it as shouting.

"Jac."

"Jac, what's she doing here?" I open the door. Yep, it's Jac, standing there with a startled look on her face. "What are you doing here?"

"When you didn't show up for the meeting, I was worried. May I come in?"

I'm still not sure what she is talking about, but I motion for her to enter. "What meeting?"

Jac is looking at me with what I can tell is a puzzled look. "Are you okay?" I see her eyes darting around the room seemingly unwilling to look at me.

I'm sure my eyes are opened wider than an owl's, as I suddenly realize what she is talking about. "God, what time is it?" My eyes squint as I try to make out the time on the radio—nine thirty. "Shit, I didn't get my wake up call. Oh, no." My hand goes to my mouth, as a vague memory of the phone ringing and my lifting the receiver then putting it back floats into my mind.

I turn around so fast that I feel myself begin to fall only to stop in mid-air, as Jac's strong arms engulf me. It is then that I realize I'm naked, and the woman who has filled my every thought for days is holding me in her arms.

I can feel a hot flush cover my face. "Guess I'd better get dressed."

Jac lets out a slight chuckle. "Actually, I kinda like you this way." Her voice is light and playful, and I struggle to figure out why she would be that way. *It's just another of her games that she plays.*

Nevertheless, I let my arms encircle Jac, and I move my lips close to hers. She offers no resistance as our lips touch tenderly before they assault each other with small sensuous kisses. As our kisses intensify and become more insistent, our tongues meet before dancing.

I am drowning in Jac—wanting nothing more than to melt into her and become one. I can feel her fingertips running up and down the exposed skin on my bare back as my need for her escalates.

"Make love with me," I whisper.

She doesn't break contact, but says, "No."

"Please, Jac...please." I am begging her and I don't care for I want her that bad.

"No, we can't."

"Why? Please, I want you."

"I want you, too, but we can't. The others are waiting for us—we need to go. It wouldn't do for us to arrive spent from making love."

Reality suddenly grips my heart and I push away from her, grabbing for the bedcover to wrap around me. "Excuses! You're filled with them. Which one will come next? I've got a headache."

"Carol, we need to talk. Will you please have dinner with me tonight? I promise to answer all your questions."

"Questions, I don't have any, Jac. You toy with me, and when I react you turn away. You've made your feelings perfectly clear. There is no need for explanations or to have dinner." Tears begin to flow without restraint. "Look at this," I say pointing to the liquid streaming down my cheeks, "I don't cry for anyone, nor do I beg. You caused this!"

Anger overtakes the passion I was feeling only moments before. "I don't know what you want from me, nor do I care anymore. I won't let that happen again for it hurts too much." I turn my back to her, as I start for the safety of the bathroom. "I need to get ready. I will be there within the hour. You can show yourself out."

Jac says, "I will wait and take you."

I close the door and hear her speaking into what I assume is the phone. "Carol is a bit under the weather. You all carry on until we get there."

✝

Arriving in the conference room, I can once again feel my face flush with embarrassment. "I am so sorry to cause everyone this delay." The others look at me, and everyone except Ron smiles.

"It's not a problem, Carol. Please take a seat and we'll get started." Jac is all business.

These are the first words I hear her speak since we left my hotel room, and I'm surprised by the compassion in her voice. I covertly look at her, as she goes through all the statistics and ideas we've developed over the last few days. Although her voice is strong and words positive, I can hear a defeated undertone. Is it because of me? She tried to talk to me and I refused to listen. What would it hurt to hear what she has to say? A pang of sadness stabs at my heart as I look at her. Tomorrow I'll head back home never knowing what she wanted to say. I know then that I can't let that happen.

In my heart, I know Jac. I can feel the rightness of that in the depths of my heart and soul. We may have only met a little over a week ago, but I know her in the most basic of ways. I have known her for all time through all the ages, of that I am certain. Where Jac is concerned, I seem to have no control. Just when I think I have broken her spell, I find myself melting with the sound of her voice or her mere presence.

Today, everyone is on their own for lunch and when we break I approach Jac. She is speaking with Ron who is fawning all over her in his ridiculous macho-man way. I feel jealous and want the scum bag to back off. I inch closer and capture Jac's eyes pleading with her to rid herself of the jerk. She only turns her attentions back to Ron and smiles sweetly.

The message she sends me is clear, and I begin to move away, knocking over a chair. *Shit, Can this day get any worse?* Regaining my composure, I look back at Jac to see a bemused expression on her face. Ron is nowhere in sight—the room is empty and she is watching me. I melt once again as my feet, seemingly with a mind of their own move in her direction. Standing only inches away from her, I can feel my heart beating uncontrollably while the warm, delicious sensation of lust fills my body.

"What time are you picking me up for dinner?" I quietly ask. "I have to warn you ahead of time, I'm not a cheap date."

The laugh is glorious. "I never thought you were, those burgers cost me a fortune."

†

Jac takes me to a small out of the way restaurant, Deux Amants, located just outside of Tyson's Corner. The tables are set apart in small, secluded alcoves, giving the diners privacy. She pulls a chair out for me and then sits in the chair next to me.

"Do you like my choice of restaurants?"

I look around the dimly lit area, appreciating the ambience and realizing exactly why we are here. "Yes, it is very intimate." I shake my head. "I like it very much."

When she looks at me with sparkling eyes, I know I am falling for her all over again—I promised myself I wouldn't.

The earlier protestations forgotten, I bask in the glow of her. She has me totally mesmerized by her presence. The level of comfort I feel when I'm around Jac is a surprise to me.

"You know, it is like I have always been with you." It takes me until we are eating dessert to have the courage to tell her that.

"I know exactly what you mean." She looks at me for what seems like ages before she speaks again. "Remember when I told you I had seen you at a conference several years ago?"

I nod wondering how different my life may have been had she actually spoken to me.

"When I opened the door, the first thing I heard was your voice and that's what drew me in. I remember your words, 'If we ignore what has happened in the past, we never will recognize what is familiar about now…' Something deep inside of me was crying out to listen to the beautiful music that your voice elicited in me. I remember thinking that I had heard you before—deep in a memory—perhaps in a dream. I knew you." She takes a long sip of her wine. "Then, when I first saw you, my heart rejoiced for it knew I had found what I had been searching for all my life."

Her words are heartfelt, and I know the truth behind them for I had much the same reaction when we first met ten days earlier. "I look at you and I have to catch my breath. I study your face as my mind tries to figure out how and where I know you from." I take her hand and hold it over my heart. "You are here and always have been."

Jac reaches out and takes my hand, oblivious to where she is or who might be watching. Slowly, she lifts it to her lips and lightly kisses each finger before speaking again. "I think it is time we go back to your room."

She never takes her eyes off me, as she takes money from her wallet and places it on the table. "Shall we go?" she asks, as she stands and offers me her hand.

Together we walk hand in hand out of the restaurant and into our future.

This time, I'm not afraid of what I am feeling.

†

I give her the key and she expertly unlocks the door. Taking the *Do Not Disturb* card off the inside handle, she places it outside then closes the door and securely locks everything.

I'm quivering inside in anticipation of the night to come. She is so beautiful. I can't believe that she actually has any interest in me or that she is about to make love with me.

Jac takes me in her arms and gently kisses my eyes and cheeks before softly placing her lips on mine. The sensations coursing through my body tell me this is so very right, and I respond to her by kissing her deeply. She pulls back a bit and smiles at me. "Are you sure?" she asks, her voice deep and sensual.

"Yes."

Her arms release me, and she begins to unbutton my shirt. With each button undone, her lips kiss the exposed skin, exploring as she makes her way to my waist. Rising up, she places her palms on my shoulders and runs them down my arms until the shirt cascades to the floor. She unfastens my bra and lets that fall, landing on my shirt.

Once again, she smiles. "You're so beautiful." Her fingertips are like feathers gliding across my body. I can feel goose bumps and know they are not from the coolness of the room but from Jac's touch. Her hands, making their way to my waist, begin to unfasten my slacks and pull the zipper down.

I want more as I stand naked in front of this incredible woman. Tentatively, I begin to remove her clothes, while Jac's fingers linger over my breasts, pulling and tugging at my taut nipples. Finally, she too is exposed, and I move into her so our bodies are touching. Explosions fill my body, as I feel myself melt into her.

We are lying in bed face to face, and Jac's thumb wipes a tear from my cheek before her lips kiss the trail left behind. "Why are you crying?"

I cannot answer her. My emotions are so raw that words have no meaning. The only response I have is to kiss her deeply before beginning to investigate her body. She responds by mirroring my every move. Lips kiss the tender skin of breasts, and tongues lavish praise on taut nipples.

I need to kiss every part of her. With each contact, my mind and body remembers more and more until I am sure, I have made love with Jac before. I find my way back to her lips and kiss her reverently. "Do you feel our connection too, Jac?"

"Yes," she whispers. "I have loved you for all time."

Our lips meet again, this time not so much in passion as in welcoming each other home. Jac is my home. She is where I belong, and I am no longer lost. I realize how alone I have felt for all my life, waiting for this moment—waiting for Jac to return to me.

"I love you."

We lay wrapped in each other's arms blissful in our love. Our love making was not the hard, heart pounding 'got to get off' type, but a slow, sensual journey of rediscovery. We became one, blending the past into the present, igniting the passions of long ago. Yes, we have found our other halves and our lovemaking reflects the joy only that discovery can bring.

I feel Jac begin to stir and make a move to leave me. "Please, don't go. Stay with me."

She lowers her body and our skin merges again. "I will always stay with you," she whispers in my ear before she kisses my lips once more.

✝

The sound of running water wakes me from a blissful sleep. Opening my eyes, I stare at the white swirled ceiling in room three-twenty-five in the Hotel Monaco in Washington DC. My body is naked, and I am sure I still feel kisses lingering everywhere as the taste and smell of Jac fills my senses. Never in my wildest imaginations could I believe anything or anyone could move me to such a passionate encounter. Yet, here I am, pulling back the soft, white sheet, letting my bare feet touch the richly carpeted floor, walking toward the bathroom, and opening the door. I can't help myself. I want—no need—to feel her luscious body next to mine again.

I stop in the doorway, shaking my head, trying to comprehend what I see. The shower is empty, the towels still neatly folded exactly where housekeeping left them.

"Where's Jac?"

Panicked, I turn back to the room and look at the bed. Only half is rumpled.

"Where's Jac?"

Then I remember—then I know. Sinking to my knees, I begin to sob uncontrollably for the pain is too real. She is gone. She was never here, and I am again alone and lost.

✝

Somehow, I pack my bags and make it to BWI. I know Jac said she'd pick me up and take me to the airport, but it

65

would be too hard to see her again. I remember how we came back to the room last night and she hugged me and kissed my cheek. I asked her to come inside and she said no. I can't understand how the passionate night we shared wasn't real.

Anyway, I'm here now. Soon, the plane will be boarding and I will be on my way home. Occasionally, I look around, hoping to see Jac with her quirky smile. Of course, in order for her to do that she'd have to care enough. *What a fool.* They call for boarding, and I am both glad and disappointed that I did not get to say good-bye to her. I need to get back to reality and my life—the one I am supposed to have, yet my heart is mourning the loss of what never could be.

When I think of the spectacle I made of myself, I feel embarrassed. I'm sure Jac must be laughing her head off. How could I be so stupid? Yet, I remember every word she said, every look she gave, and every touch on my body. All of that pulled me in, and I know she felt it too—our connection, our past, and our love. Now, I have let her go and I am sure there will be many days of self-loathing and nights of endless tears that she will never hear.

Chapter Seven

That night after arriving home, I'm finding it difficult to smile. I draw into myself feigning an upset stomach from something I ate on the plane and go to bed. Every time I open or close my eyes, Jac is there filling my mind with both sadness and joy. I know Mike is worried about me, but how can I tell him what has happened or what I feel? He has been so good to me over the years, and I wonder, not for the first time, what it would have been like if it was Jac instead.

For the rest of the weekend, I mope around the house trying to give the appearance of normality when I feel a devastation that has no bounds. My heart cries out for what I've lost. How could life be so cruel to show me what I hadn't known I'd lost only to take it away from me? The words over our last dinner together haunt me for it was clear that Jac had the same feelings as I did. Her revelations about when she first saw me proved that. Then why did she let me go?

There is no doubt that for the rest of my life my heart will be crying for what was lost to me. For a moment in time, I had a glimpse of what was and what could be. In those moments with Jac, I knew a happiness and joy unlike any other in my life. I am forever changed, and I know that only Jac will make my heart smile again. For now, I must go through the motions of living for my family's sake for they have done nothing but be loving and supportive toward me. Jac is gone and they are here.

†

Monday morning doesn't come fast enough. I need to distance myself from Mike and the worried, hurt concern in his eyes and on his face. I know he deserves an explanation for my actions but I don't have the words to explain it to myself much less someone else.

I drag myself into work earlier than usual. I welcome the quiet and the chance to be alone. I sit down at my desk and go through all the neatly stacked messages. I mindlessly look at them not really paying attention until one grabs my attention.

Jacqueline Reinhart would like you to call her as soon as you arrive back. I check the time and see it was early Friday. "Probably wants my report," I say to the piece of pink paper. Continuing on, I find four more messages from Jac. The last one reads, *Jacqueline Reinhart called again and really needs to speak with you as soon as possible.*

"Fat chance of that happening. I've learned my lesson and will never let her hurt me again." I crumble up all her messages and throw them exactly where they belong—in the trash. All the while, my heart is crying out for the connection to her.

I sigh deeply when I look at the time and realize that soon everyone will be coming to work. It will be show time and I am not certain I can pull it off without crying. Over the years, I have managed to put a wall around my emotions. Until Jac came into my life, I was very adept at hiding my feelings. Now, I'm not sure I will ever be able to do that again.

Next, I start to go through my mail. I see a special delivery letter with the name J. Reinhart as the sender. "Mailed on Friday...she must have sent it by courier. Wow! That must have cost a fortune."

Instantly, I begin to open it to see what she has to say, only to stop myself. Holding the envelope, I want desperately to tear it into tiny pieces, yet I long to know what she has written, hoping for a reason to break the hold she has over me. Opening it, I see the clear, bold writing that I know is Jac's.

My Dearest Carol,

What do I say to you? Your leaving without waiting devastated me. I know I sent you mixed signals all week and that you felt rejected by me when you reacted to what you thought those signals meant. It wasn't you, Carol. It was my fear of the deep love I feel for you. I told you, I had found what I had been searching for all my life and that is the truth. I know you felt the sincerity behind those words. I could see it in your eyes. I also saw the love there and frankly, that scares me.

Each time I found myself drawn to you and wanting to show you how much I love you, I turned away. I'm not sure I can explain why, but I want to try.

If we made love, I don't think I would be able to let you go back to your life and not resent everything and everyone that is part of you. I think if had I asked, you would have stayed. Your life is not with me and to take you away from what you know and love would have been wrong. Had you remained with me, we would have been blissfully happy, of that I am certain. But, I would wait in fear for the day that you would resent me for taking you away from your family. It would be a birthday, a holiday, or a phone call that would remind you of what you gave up and the resentment would start. I know how much your family means to you and know that day would surely come.

Do you recall one of our discussions and my telling you how much I detest liars? Do you know why? Of course you don't. I was in a relationship for close to sixteen years. I would still be there except I came home one day and found someone else in my bed. When I think back on all the lies and farfetched stories I convinced myself were true, I cringe at my stupidity.

Can you understand if we made love, we would have been no better than that which I deplore? I can't and won't do that to you, Carol. I love you too much to put you through that kind of heartache.

This is not our lifetime—at least not right now. I'm sorry that I hurt you so badly and was unable to explain my actions more effectively. But, I feel it was for the best for us both.

You are in my heart now and for always. I love you. I always have and always will. I am always here for you.

Yours forever,
Jac

My heart is breaking as I realize the truth in her words. She let me go because she loves me. If she had asked, I would have left everything I know and love behind, to spend the rest of my life with her. She is my heart and soul. I am certain that I lost her in another lifetime and have been searching for her ever since. How ironic that now that we have found each other again, we must let go. Her words are poignant and the truth behind them too real to ignore.

I know that in every lifetime, souls search for their mate longing to be complete once again. Sometimes they pass each other with instant recognition; while other times only a nanosecond lies between, a chance meeting that never happens. Souls destined to meet must seize the moment or it will pass them by, leaving them searching in vain.

I must be satisfied knowing where Jac is and that the loneliness that my soul felt is gone. I have no right to expect anything from her. All I can give her is my heart and that will have to be enough.

Picking up the phone, I dial her number.

"Hello."

I hear her voice and I am no longer lost, I am found. My search is over, for I have found my other half—I am complete. "Hi, it's me."

Chapter Eight

Jac—Seduction

As I stand here in the back of the very auditorium where I first saw Carol, I can still hear her voice from all those years ago. I recall that, at that moment, every fiber of my being was screaming as I listened to her speech and when I saw her, I knew I had come home.

Why didn't I make Carol my own and bed her when I had the chance last year? It was what we both wanted, yet I held back, unable to take that final step. I've asked myself that question a million times since I last saw her. Oh, I still have contact with her over the phone but not in person. I don't think my resolve would last if I were close to her again. The urge to touch her would be too great.

I realize just how much I lost by choosing not to take her for my own. My life has been sad and lonely ever since. Standing here alone, I am trying to figure out what happened in my life to bring me to this point. Carol will be here in less than an hour, and I need to understand everything before I can take the next step and rectify my mistake.

✝

I was born Jacqueline Marie Reinhart, the baby in a family of four children. My mother nicknamed me Jaci, pronounced Jackie, because she said it sounded the same but by spelling it differently; it gave me a distinction from everyone else. I thought it was dumb, but what's a kid gonna do? So I held on to the ridiculous spelling until I went away to college where I quickly became Jac.

Early on, I realized the power of intelligence married to charm and used it constantly to my advantage. When I was eight months old I began walking, and I am pretty sure a week later I was running, 'cause I've never stopped or looked back. At the time, I thought life was too delicious to waste time on what was.

I remember in grade school being the most popular kid and the pleasure I got from seeing the looks on the other kids faces when everyone wanted me to be on their team and would always pick me first. There was a mixture of happiness, envy, and hate on some of the other's faces. I learned to put on a happy face and let everyone think that they were more important to me than they really were. Even then, I was a master of manipulation.

All through those years, I can remember people commenting on how grounded and nice I was and how I didn't realize my beauty or charm. Yeah, right. If they only knew the real me that I never let anyone else see. They wouldn't have any positive thoughts about me. It was all just a show of smoke and mirrors, for deep inside I thrived on being number one and watching others suffer for it. It was narcissism at its best.

Even now…I chew my lips…that Carol is in my life, I at times still enjoy watching others flounder in my wake. She has changed me you know. She really has. It's just that old ways are hard to let go of, but I'm making headway. As I look around this empty auditorium, I feel bereft for all the opportunities I missed by not being a better person when it counted.

I always knew I was more interested in women sexually than men. I can remember, in school, all the girls going gaga over this or that actor or singer, and secretly inside my eyes were set on the starlet or the sexy woman songstress. Of course, no one knew. After all, I was a master of deception and skilled at hiding my true feelings.

†

My family had a vacation home on a small lake that we called "The Upper Forty." We would go there every chance we could, and the summers would find my mother, sisters, brother, and me staying full time, with my father commuting on the weekends. I fondly remember what wonderful times those were.

I was sixteen the summer of my first 'lesbian' encounter. Both my brother and sister had summer jobs, and my two-year-old sister occupied my mother most days, unless she needed to go out and then I had to babysit. Fortunately, that wasn't very often.

Sally Jansen and her family had bought the house next door to ours. From the moment I saw her, I knew by the way she acted that we were on the same wavelength. She liked me and I certainly liked her.

Sally had bright-red hair, which I suspected others would tease to no end, calling her 'woody' or 'red.' She was about two inches shorter than my five nine, with a body that, although not fat, was not particularly lean or muscular. Her face was full of freckles that often reminded me of my idea of what Huckleberry Finn or Tom Sawyer looked like. I have to laugh now when I think of her. Of course, at the time, she

74

was better looking to me than any boy in reality or fiction. Soon we became fast friends—I wanted her sexually so that meant friendship to me. I had always been used to getting my way and taking her wouldn't be any different. I knew she didn't stand a chance.

I introduced her to my lake friends, and we would often all hang out together swimming, boating, skiing, and getting into trouble. When our parents were away, we would all meet up and have a party. Oh, those parties were the stuff that legends are made of. Sally fit in perfectly. At one of the parties, we all played a game of dare. One of Sally's dares was to kiss a girl. I knew she would pick me 'cause everyone always did. Her lips were so soft, and the kiss had my hormones screaming for more. Of course I protested, but the look in Sally's eyes said that she wanted more.

I can still feel the memory of my first time invade my body.

I remember how hot and bright the day was. We all decided to meet up on my swimming dock after dinner to knock back a few beers. Tony Pagallia was there along with Sally, Chrissy Baldwin, Kevin Holman, and Ronnie Blankenship. The beer flowed freely, and we were all laughing and kidding around when Tony picked me up and jumped into the water with me in his arms. I am sure all the other kids were shocked when this happened, as no one had ever dared fool with me like that before. After all, I was Jaci, the one everyone wanted to be with and be like. No one dared to incur my wrath, and it certainly seemed as though Tony was doing just that.

As I surfaced, I screamed out, "What the hell are you doing to me, Tony?" I was pissed and looked around to see his face all smiling and full of amusement. I shook my head so that my long, light-brown hair created a spray of water.

"You look sexy when you do that." Tony came closer to me, and I remember a growl forming deep inside me.

While treading the water to keep myself upright, I lifted my hand out of the water and slapped his face. "Never do that to me again," I screamed.

Undaunted, he wrapped his arms around me and began kissing me. I know I heard a collective gasp from the onlookers on the dock. I struggled to get free, then I began slapping him repeatedly. "Don't you ever touch me again," I screamed. With strong strokes, I swam for the ladder and climbed up onto the dock.

Tony continued to tread water and, for some reason, his face still showed amusement. His friend Ronnie, standing on the dock with his hands on his hips, was laughing. "Man, what the hell did you do that for? Shit you must be drunk or something."

It didn't take long after that for everyone but Sally and I to pile into Kevin's boat, give us hasty waves, and head away from the dock.

It seemed as though Sally could feel my anger, because she kept trying to comfort me. There was no way I'd let her see just how pissed off I was. No, I was planning my revenge. Sweetly of course. Tony would pay for his violation of me. He would pay dearly, I would see to that. By the time the summer was over, all our friends believed Tony was into guys. All it took was a few well-placed comments and, suddenly, Tony roughhousing with the guys took on a whole new meaning.

That was the first time anyone had challenged me, and I could feel my body churning with anger and indignation. I could feel the warmth of Sally's body as she sat close to me. I can remember swallowing hard when her thigh lightly touched mine. Want began to replace the rage I was feeling.

Our eyes met and I saw what I now know as the familiar *want* in her eyes. I leaned into her and kissed her waiting lips. She returned the kiss, and soon we were sharing our first real intimate kiss. Suddenly, I heard the roar of a boat off in the distance and broke the kiss.

Our eyes locked and I took her hand. "Let's go somewhere more private," I whispered.

We both jumped in the water and began swimming the hundred yards or so back to the boat dock on the shore. Once we reached the ladder on the dock, we stopped and there, under the pilings, we kissed again.

I can still remember those lips and my first real kisses. I was behind her as we climbed up the ladder and the swaying of her hips mesmerized me. I thought I would explode. Once inside the boathouse, we fell into each other's arms, our kisses getting deeper and more powerful. Soon, we lay on a tarp that we used for covering the boat in the winter. Our bodies ground together as kisses found their way to ears, necks, and other exposed parts of our bodies. I wanted her, and I took the next logical step—I began to untie her bikini top.

"Stop," she said, as she took my arm and pushed it away before moving away from me.

I was confused but stopped. "Why," I asked her. "Don't you want this?"

"This is wrong." She was heading for the door.

I put my hormones in check, and I looked at her with my anger rising. I wanted her. Now that I look back on it, I didn't want her particularly as much as I wanted the experience. "If you walk away don't bother to ever come back, Sally."

She left, and I was already planning how to get back at her. I knew I had the power of persuasion in getting my way, and I knew of her insecurities. I would play on them to get my way and exactly what I wanted from her. For the next week, I wouldn't talk to her or have anything to do with her. It didn't take long for her to come around to my way of thinking.

The first time we had sex we were in the boathouse again, where we fashioned a makeshift bed. We both fumbled with clothes and finding where hands, legs, and bodies fit best. My, did I enjoy myself. I guess Sally did too, but that really wasn't my concern. My active imagination and avid reading led Sally to accuse me of having had sex before. "Jaci, you told me you never did this before," I remember her screaming.

After pulling her near again I whispered, "Darlin' you are my first and are such an inspiration that I surprised even myself."

She pushed me away. "I need to go, my folks will be wondering where I am."

I watched her dressing with the light streaming through the boathouse window silhouetting her body. I wanted more and was determined to get what I wanted. Standing and moving close to her, I stroked her face and began kissing her neck. "We have plenty of time." I began moving my lips close to hers before capturing them between my teeth.

"Jaci, we can't."

I laughed, for her protests were weak and before I knew it, she was kissing my lips hard. I smiled inwardly knowing that she would do my bidding and be a willing participant whenever and wherever I wanted her.

By the end of summer, Sally was professing her love for me, wanting to know when and where we could see each other again.

I smiled my sweetest smile at her. "Never," was my answer.

A look of panic crossed her face. "You don't mean that. Not after all we've meant to each other."

I watched as she looked at my face searching it for a different answer.

"Noooo, you can't do this. I love you."

I can still remember shaking my head and laughing at her derisively. She had walked away from me that first time and now she'd have to pay. "Sally, the summer is over and we had a great time together, but it is time we both move on." Her sobs became wails, and I moved in to stop her. "Listen, you're off to your school and I'm off to mine. Can't you see that we have different lives and it will never work?" Then I moved in, lifted her face, and wiped her tears away with my thumbs. "Sally, you are so beautiful. You deserve someone better than me. Someone who will share your life, love you, and make you happy."

Her watery blue eyes were pleading with me. "We can make it work, Jaci. I love you so much. Please."

"But, I don't love you. I don't even know what love is." I pulled her closer and held her tight while stroking her hair. "Sally, you know I'm right, don't you?"

I felt her head shake.

"What do you say I give you a call when I get home? Maybe we can meet." I did not intend to see her ever again, but this would placate her until my family left the lake for the summer.

"Really. You will? Oh, Jaci, I know we can make it work somehow." She was elated.

That was my cue to have my way with her one last time, and I made sure it was so explosive that I was leaving her wanting more. It was then that I discovered the power sexual encounters could have for me.

I never did call her and the next summer, when she arrived, I blew her off and never spoke to her again. Yes, it was cruel, but she had served her usefulness to me and that was all I really cared about back then. That was until Carol came into my life.

Chapter Nine

In college, I became 'Jac' and found a completely new world open before me. The women were numerous and so pliable that I found myself inventing games on how to lure straight women into my bed. It was so easy. They all thought forever. Yeah, right. Forever was a word that didn't belong in my vocabulary,

After I graduated, I was able to get a job with a small, urban social services organization. Being who I was, I knew I could make a difference in the lives of all I touched. During that time, I came to realize that if I was going to really succeed and make a difference I needed to do more. Learn more. Make better contacts and choices.

I know—how could someone like me who is so narcissistic actually be interested in the betterment of mankind or anyone else for that matter? When I was growing up, I used to talk with Audrey Conklin, the lady next door. She always seemed interested in me and, besides, as I got older I realized just how cute she was. Beautiful is probably more appropriate.

Anyway, when I was thirteen I went over to her house to return her punch bowl my mom had borrowed. As was my habit, I just walked in for I had been doing that for most of my life. I found her sitting at the kitchen table sobbing into her hands.

I remember asking her what was wrong. She didn't answer and buried her face deeper.

I placed the bowl tentatively on the table next to her and turned to leave, but something held me there. I went back to the table and I gave her a hug, which was completely out of character for me. It just seemed the right thing to do at the time. She looked up at me, and I saw her deeply bruised face that seemed to be pleading with me to stay.

I sat down.

I remember looking at her and noticing that her arms had purple finger marks. *Big fingers* was all I could think. It seemed to me that I sat there for hours with a woman who had always treated me with kindness, and I knew that someone had beaten her badly. It probably was only a short time, but in that moment, something happened to me that had never happened before. I felt her pain.

Six weeks later, they found her broken and battered body in her living room after the police received a domestic violence call. She died three days later.

I vowed I would do whatever I could to see that never happened again. I can still hear the wailing of the ambulance's sirens as they carried her away. It just wasn't right, and I wanted to do something that would make a difference. At first, I thought law enforcement, but I realized that they only came along after the fact. I needed to be there before it happened to make sure it didn't. This is something that I feel passionate about, and all my narcissism goes out the window where my work is concerned.

That's where I am coming from. It was during my first job that I decided the best way to make a difference was to get into a government agency. They were, after all, the policy makers, and I felt that through tough comprehensive standards, social workers could have the tools to make a difference and save lives—to save the Audrey Conklin's of the world. If I was going to do that I needed to go back to school and get higher degrees, so I enrolled in graduate school.

†

Now, I don't want you to think that during this time I lived a celibate life. Far from it. Very far from it. I dated many and bedded many more, but it wasn't until I met Casey Higgins that I finally decided to settle down. Casey and I dated on and off while I was working on my thesis for my PhD. She was working on her masters in social work, so we did have something in common. That didn't happen too often with most of the women I dated. To be frank, the first thing that attracted me to her was her father.

No, I wasn't interested in him. He held a high-level government job, and he would be my perfect *in* to get the job I coveted at the Department of Health and Human Services. As callous as it sounds to me now, Casey was the means to an end.

If I hadn't found out about her father's connections, I doubt that I would have even noticed her. She was rather plain looking with straggly hair and a soft body. After I got to know her, I found her to be a kind, gentle woman who had a good heart. When I was thirty-two, I asked her to move in with me and become my partner. She readily agreed and, six months later, her father arranged for me to get a job in a mid-level position at HHS. Life was good.

Casey was a good partner. She cleaned, cooked, and even did the ironing. I couldn't ask for more. She was nothing special in bed, but I didn't mind, for I could always find a fiery and willing bedmate when I was out of town and that was often enough to fulfill my needs.

Faithful was not a word in my vocabulary then. At that time, I wanted to get ahead. I had my sights set on being the head of HHS, and I was a woman in a man's world. The only way to get noticed, if I had a chance at the job, was to work twenty-four seven. I liked coming home to a hot meal, clean house, clean sheets, and a smiling face, so my arrangement with Casey was perfect. She was malleable enough, and I knew she would always be there. After all, I was Jac and always got what and whom I wanted.

†

We had been living together for ten years, when an opportunity came up for us both to attend the same conference in Dallas. I was to be a keynote speaker, and Casey was interested in attending one of the workshops with new and innovative ideas for social workers. The past year of our relationship had been rocky for us. Casey began demanding more and more of my time, and I was unwilling to give it to her. I liked things the way they were and did not intend to change anything, especially for her.

I had hoped that the trip to Dallas would give me the opportunity to cajole her into seeing things my way. After all, she would have my undivided attention for five full days and that was what she wanted. For me, it would be difficult to satisfy her needs for my time when we returned home but I would try. I was used to her and liked all that she did for me. I guess, in some way, I loved her as much as I could. I know she loved me and that was what made it so difficult.

I remember how pleased she was when we entered our hotel suite. She beamed because she thought she had me all to herself and, to be truthful, that is what I intended. Really it was. I had no idea that my life would change forever there in Dallas, Texas. I didn't see it coming, and it took me by surprise when it happened.

It all started out innocently enough. The day had come for my speech, and I was engrossed in preparations for that when Casey tried to interrupt my chain of thought, babbling about something I had no interest in.

"Jac, I want to catch the lecture in Auditorium B," Casey told me. I knew she was trying to get my attention, but I ignored her. "Are you listening to me?"

I listened to the drone of her voice while trying to concentrate on the notes for my speech. Finally, she tugged on my arm. "I said, are you listening to me?"

"Yes, I'm listening. If I am going to be prepared for my speech, I need to finish this, Casey. You know how important this is to me, so can you give me a minute?"

"Take all the time you need, Jac. I'm heading over there now." She was opening the door. "Come and find me when you're done," she said over her shoulder as the door shut.

Although Casey's words sounded understanding, I'd been with her long enough to know she was seething. As hard as I tried, I knew that this trip wasn't working out the way she'd planned. The demands on my time were such that I couldn't wine and dine her every moment, and that was a major problem. She was on me all the time, whining that I wasn't spending enough time with her. It was obvious that she didn't understand the responsibilities or the importance of the keynote speaker at the event. In the three days that we'd been in Dallas, her demeanor had become so bitchy that I hated to be around her.

85

Actually, it probably was my fault. What I wanted was to be actively engaged in what was happening at the convention. The last thing I wanted was to be stuck with only her. I know that doesn't sound nice, but at the time it was important for me to be out there listening and understanding what the attendees were saying about their jobs. If I was going to come up with a plan to revamp the system, I needed to know the lay of the land so to speak.

As for Casey, nothing that I did seemed to make her happy anymore and, at that moment, I'd had all of the whining that I could take. Nevertheless, I did care for her and really didn't want anything to change permanently. So, my plan was to do what I could to make our relationship work. I finished the review of my notes, and I headed to the auditorium where I knew Casey would be. I remember thinking that maybe after my speech we could have an early dinner and then spend the night in each other's arms. It had been a long time since we'd made love.

†

Opening the door to the auditorium, I heard "If we ignore what has happened in the past, we never will recognize what is familiar about now..." The voice was like music to my ears, beckoning me to the owner. In the dim light, I fixed my eyes on the brightly illuminated speaker. Tingles seared my body, as somewhere in the deepest recesses of my soul there was no doubt that I knew her. I was mesmerized by the stranger and stood against the back wall of the room, spellbound, before making my way down the aisle to sit as close to her as I could.

The woman next to me glared at me as if I was intruding in her space. I remember thinking that whoever the speaker was she must have cast her spell on the others too.

Finally, she stopped speaking and began fielding questions. The hands raised were numerous, and the woman deftly answered each one. I wished I had something to ask her, but for the life of me, I couldn't think of anything to say, which was unusual for me. The questions ended and attendees instantly surrounded her. With my eyes fixed on her, I made my way toward the front of the auditorium. I wanted, no needed, to speak with the woman.

At last, I was standing there close enough to her to feel the heat of her body. I could see her face clearly and my heart skipped a beat, as I knew in my soul that I was where I was supposed to be. I knew her. There was no doubt that we had been one in the past. The feelings were so overwhelming that I felt dizzy and exhilarated at the same time. She was the one. Definitely the one.

Tentatively, I reached out to touch her when I heard, "Jac, there you are. I said B not D. Don't you ever listen to me?"

The bitch is back was all I could think. I could feel my eyes rolling as I turned around and saw Casey standing there. Her presence didn't register in my brain, and I turned back to the woman only to see her retreating back. I felt bereft. The feeling of euphoria I'd had only moments before became one of great sorrow. The strong memory of "what was" shook me to my core, and I was lost in the wonder of it.

Once again, I heard Casey speaking, but I didn't seem to understand her words. Finally, I felt a hand on my shoulder as it firmly spun me around.

"What is going on with you?" she demanded. "I've been standing here talking to you, and you act as if I don't exist. Some great vacation you dragged me on. Why are you in this auditorium?"

I knew I was looking at Casey and hearing her words, but for the life of me, they seemed like a foreign language. "Do you know who that woman who just spoke is?" I ask.

"How the hell would I know?" Her voice is grating on my nerves. "She's probably some nobody that is just filling up time. Why does it matter to you?"

Those words I did hear, and rage toward the woman who'd shared my life for ten years rose up in me. "You are wrong, Casey. She was definitely somebody. Had you been here to listen you would have heard a very powerful speaker with an equally powerful message." I bent over and picked up a discarded program.

Carol Barngate: Lessons of the Past — A look at how we can use past events to predict the outcome of abuse. The ethical and emotional support for battered women.

I read the name again, envisioning her face and hearing her voice. I knew I must find her and speak to her for there was no doubt that she was my future.

"Jac, are you coming or not?"

Casey's grating voice made me feel like I had just gotten aluminum foil between my teeth. "Yeah, I'm right behind you." All notions of a romantic night were gone.

Chapter Ten

Once I returned to DC and my office, I made it my mission to find out all about Carol Barngate. Being in the position I was in made it rather easy to track her down. It was then that I began my preparations for meeting, bedding, and making one Carol Barngate mine. That was what I meant to do. Funny how plans sometimes go on a different track than the one you expected.

Her credentials were first rate, and I wasn't surprised to learn she had quite a good reputation among other social workers. She had written many papers analyzing methods and practices that made the job social workers do more tedious and less effective. I read everything repeatedly. I was so haunted and consumed by her that I couldn't eat or sleep. Casey, of course, noticed and would harp on me all the time about closing her out. "If you'd only let me in, Jac. I'm not the enemy you know," she'd say. How could I let her in? What would I say? *I found the one and you're not her.*

I needed a plan—a way of bringing Carol Barngate into my life. For days, I pondered how to make it happen, when suddenly it was there staring me right in the face. My plans for redesigning the system along with her concepts of making the job work for the clients. It was perfect. Of course, I needed a working plan to redesign everything and that took years.

My mission had become Carol Barngate and nothing would stand in my way. Casey and I finally drifted apart two years later. I really didn't care, for she was no longer part of the equation. We'd go through the routine of our lives, living together, and although she tried to make it work. It didn't.

One day, I came home early to pick up a journal I had left behind and found Casey in my bed with some woman I vaguely recalled from the gym we'd joined. I probably should have gotten mad or shown that it somehow mattered to me but I didn't. Instead, I turned around and walked out the door. Later, I called and told her to be gone before I got home. I had stopped caring years before.

†

After years of preparation, my plan was finally ready for activation. By that time, I knew all there was to know about Carol Barngate. Everything from her home address, her bank accounts, and even to the perfume she used. Chanel. That was her fragrance, and I would spray the pillow each night with the scent I knew was hers. I also knew that every Wednesday she would have lunch at a small Italian restaurant named Vinny's with her friend, Evelyn Delarosa. That detail would factor into my plan so I could innocently meet Carol.

The first person I contacted was the county executive, whom I approached with the idea of one of his health workers cooperating with the HHS in streamlining the social services system. Of course, he was interested. Why shouldn't he be? It was a feather in his cap. I purposely set up a meeting with the county executive, Edgar Blankenship; the director of health services, Oscar Barony; and his assistant, Evelyn Delarosa for a Wednesday morning. I knew, without a doubt, that I would be able to charm my way into having lunch with the Delarosa woman and Carol Barngate.

The meeting was interesting, as the exec strutted about puffing himself up with self-importance and implications that the whole thing was his idea. The director was not much better, but at least he listened to what I had to say. I made eye contact with Evelyn as if to say "help me," and she responded with a smile. Oh, I had to play it cool and not let her in on what my real intentions were. It was fortunate for me that the Delarosa woman was easy to manipulate. "Of course, I would have lunch with her," and "oh how sorry I was to intrude on her plans." That had been my plan, after all, and it was working perfectly.

Panic doesn't even begin to describe what I felt when I walked into Vinny's. I spoke casually with the proprietor, all the while my eyes covertly following Evelyn's progress toward my goal. Seeing Carol sitting there smiling fondly at her friend set millions of butterflies all flapping their wings at once in my stomach. Oh, I was acting so very casual, lingering in my conversation with the man, all the while surreptitiously watching Carol. For the first time in my life, I was feeling unsure of myself.

When our eyes actually met, I was lost in the warm glow of her dark emerald eyes. I extended my hand to her, and when she took it every nerve ending in my body exploded with excitement. I had actually met my quarry, and inside I was doubtful of the abilities I had been so sure of all my life. But, I did regain my composure and put on the charm that has gotten me far in life. Once again, it didn't let me down.

When you long for something and then get it, there is always the possibility that it will never live up to the fantasy you've created. Not so with Carol. Although it was our first encounter, it was as if we had known each other forever. I couldn't believe it. All my life, I was always the user, the player who never let anyone in to see the real me. For me, the hunt and the game were foremost and the individuals involved in my sport unimportant. Yet, there I was sitting with this remarkable woman, feeling completely naked and open. Even more surprising, it didn't seem to bother me or send off alarms of self-protection.

Still, the game was on. I recognized in her eyes the want and the need, for I had seen it before. I knew that she would be mine; it was just a matter of the right time and place. Oh, I played it to the hilt, manipulating every situation to my advantage. When we hadn't eaten our lunch, I made plans with her to have dinner. I knew she was married and would have to make a choice, but I was confident I would win. I am not proud of what I did next, for it was cruel, but that was how I had lived my life. At that moment, it seemed the right thing to do.

I had told Carol I would call her after my meeting with the exec and other officials and set up a time and place for dinner. When the meeting ran over, I could have called her, but I felt a power play was in order so I blew her off. I can remember standing and looking out the window of the conference room and seeing Carol crossing the street toward the parking garage. Inwardly, I was smiling, because I knew at that moment I was in charge. She would go home wondering what had happened, why I didn't call, especially after her friend Evelyn had already left.

I knew her home number and could have called her there, but I wanted her to spend the night thinking about me, agonizing over the lost opportunity, and wanting me. I left a message at her work number, knowing that once she heard it all bad thoughts about me would end and her interest in me would pique her even more. I had played this game a thousand times. Why would I play it any differently with her? Carol deserved better, and I knew that in my heart, but I wasn't into listening to my heart. I hadn't in the past, so my reasoning was: "why should I begin paying attention now?" Flawed, I know, but I was a different person then.

The game was on, and I played it to perfection. She would be mine, of that I was certain. I had taken women away from men before, and Carol's situation didn't bother me at all. Although, I do remember feeling twinges of jealousy when she received the flowers from her husband. It was such an odd feeling, for I had never felt jealous of anyone or anything in my life. Looking back, I can now see that she was the first person to change this narcissist into a real, caring person. Well, she actually wasn't the first—my neighbor, Audrey, was but that was different. Audrey gave me a purpose where Carol, I later realized, gave me life.

†

The game was going perfectly. I wanted her to have the best, so I arranged for her to have a room in the Hotel Monaco on Capitol Hill at my expense. I, of course, had the room next to hers, but she didn't know that for it was all part of the game.

I picked her up at the airport, and it was there that I made my first move when I gave her a big hug then took her arm as we walked to the baggage claim area. When she didn't rebuke my advances, I knew my objective was in sight. When I asked her if she was ready to go and her response was, "Yes, ready to go with you anywhere," I knew all I needed to do was reel her in, and I would do just that after the symphony.

Once we arrived at the hotel, I was pleased to see she liked the suite. It was then that the game got interesting, as she began to flirt with me. I have had women come on to me enough to know when they are interested in more. Even though I'd pursued her all those years and felt a connection, it was still a game to me. Carol was no exception. I remember inwardly smiling in victory, but when we kissed for the first time, something strange happened to me. All the cavalier notions I'd had about bedding women flew out the window. It was the first time in my life that I cared that what I was doing wasn't very nice or honorable.

For me, it had always been about the game and the win—most importantly the win. I had never entered an encounter where I felt anything for the other person except lust. Yet, when her lips touched mine, my whole body reacted not in desire but in a feeling that I had never felt before. Peace invaded my entire being. It was beautiful.

With that one kiss, I knew she was mine, although I didn't realize at the time how much I wanted that to be. I could tell she wanted more, and it would have been so easy to take her without delay, but something held me back. I remember thinking to myself that *there is always tonight after the symphony*. I wonder if I had known then there would never be a *tonight*, would I have acted at that moment and taken her? Actually, knowing what I do now, I am glad I didn't act, for it would have meant the never ending cycle would continue.

I had spent five years developing a way to find, meet, and bed Carol Barngate. Just when victory was at hand, I dropped the ball. I didn't choke or fall in love and become all noble and selfless. No, that didn't happen, well, at least not the noble and selfless part. I did fall in love with Carol from the moment I'd first heard her voice. So, why didn't I claim my love? Why didn't I steal her away from her husband and make her my own? I did what I did because when you do the right thing you only have one choice. Our love at that time could never be, and I knew that as sure as I knew she was the one.

Chapter Eleven

Our dinner date had been wonderful, and for the first time we shared that we found the other familiar as though we had met before. I had told her about seeing her in Dallas at the SWOA and how I knew her first by her voice. A song about meeting someone and knowing them kept running through my mind, but for the life of me, I couldn't find the words. I knew if I could sing it, everything I was feeling would be explained. The lyrics evaded me.

We were sitting next to each other, listening to the plaintive sounds of the *Pastoral* by Beethoven. From time to time through the performance, Carol would reach over and touch my arm or hand. Once, she touched me and all kinds of bells and whistles set off inside my brain. My body was on high alert, and I craved to feel her body next to mine only to suddenly have the strangest feeling come over me. I was in a dream, and Carol was calling out to me and holding out her hand, begging me to claim her.

It was in that moment that I knew we had done this before, many times. As I sat there with Carol's hand lightly resting on mine, knowing that I was going to make her my own that night. A terror struck my heart and panic invaded my mind. All the past lives of my taking Carol away from another to make her mine were flooding into my brain. Then there was something else—disaster, death, and bereavement. Suddenly, I understood the game. I understood how I needed to play it, for I had played it many times before with Carol. As the music reached a crescendo, I felt myself shaking inside. When I heard the lamenting sounds of the symphony's familiar theme I knew what had to be done and what I needed to do to make things right.

There was no doubt that if I continued the cycle, Carol and I would be lovers in this lifetime but doomed to repeat the mistake in future lifetimes. In all our past lives, I had taken what wasn't mine to take, leaving me to spend lifetimes of reiterating the same scenario until I got it right. The first words I heard Carol speak echoed in my mind, *"If we ignore what has happened in the past, we never will recognize what is familiar about now..."* and I understood what those words mean, not only to me, but to her as well. We had walked the path before, yet we—or me, most likely me—had never recognized the mistake until it was too late.

I remember wondering to myself just how many lifetimes we had wasted because of my bravado and stupid insistence on having things my way. In some ways, I think fate brought me to that auditorium at the exact moment Carol spoke those words. Somewhere in the universe, cosmic tumblers were trying to tell me to listen to her words and learn from them. I think that is why I never forgot them and why from time to time they would haunt my subconscious. A lesson was there to learn if I would only listen.

Once I understood the powerful message, I knew I could never take Carol away from her family. Somewhere deep inside me, I knew that sharing the message with Carol would be a mistake. She had to find it out on her own, or we would be destined to repeat this life into millennium. The problem then was how to stop what I had started—the seduction of Carol.

After the symphony, we returned to her room. She invited me in for a drink and I obliged her, because although I knew we would not make love, I still needed to feel close to her. I know it was selfish, but I was weak. We kissed and it took all the strength I could muster to turn away and leave her there wanting more. Instead of going to my room that was next door, I continued on to the elevator and out of the hotel.

I needed relief and went to a local lesbian bar. Once inside, I found myself searching for a Carol look alike but soon realized that only the real thing would do. It was so ironic that for the first time in my life I found myself feeling loyalty to someone. I left the bar and headed back to the hotel. I found a dark corner in the bar there. All my carefully laid plans were unraveling. For the first time in my life, I was at a loss as to how to make anything work to my advantage. I was considering another's feelings, and that was foreign to me.

Once back in my room, I arranged for Carol's breakfast, undressed, and flopped into bed. Although the walls in the old building were thick and soundproof, I swore I could hear Carol sobbing. I remember thinking that I was responsible and wondering how I was ever going to undo the harm I had done.

†

I recall standing in a conference room at the Department of Health and Human Services as the most pleasurable feeling invaded my body. Carol was there. I knew it, and when I found her beautiful dark emerald eyes, I knew I was home. Her gaze pierced through all my defenses until it came to rest on my inner most being and I was not afraid. I welcomed her with an open heart.

Throughout the day, I found myself drawn to her and would often pass by her and reach out and touch a shoulder, back, or arm. I needed to feel the connection, but mostly I needed to feel. My heart had found what it had been aching for. I realized that all the games, posturing, and blustering of my life was a sham to hide the emptiness of my soul.

That night, we went to a local night spot called Madam's Organ along with all the other symposium attendees. In reality, I wanted to spend the time with Carol only, but since I was in charge, it was important that I make all the members feel important. When that slime ball Ron Cuthbert made the gesture to sit next to me, I felt revulsion. Throughout the night, he leered at me and shot daggers at Carol.

Carol certainly put him in his place. Her abilities at playing and winning their little card game forced her to drink seven shots. I remember marveling at how well she could hold her liquor. I knew that the drinking would give me a perfect excuse for not taking her to bed. I know that I hurt her, for she saw my refusal to make love with her as a sign of rejection.

I remember after she stormed away from my car that I sat there for a long while before I finally parked and went into the hotel. I went to her door, wanting desperately to see her and explain this connection and past lives. It had been so easy for me to accept but would she? Most probably, she would think it an elaborate ruse. I hung my head, listening helplessly to her sobs, and my heart and body ached with regret and sorrow. I wanted nothing more than to knock and take her as my own, but I knew that could not happen. Not then. Not ever.

Being noble is hell.

†

All I wanted was to while away the hours with Carol, even if she thought me a jerk. It was necessary to conduct the business that I had brought everyone together for. The next day was all business, as everyone broke down into pairs to tackle different aspects of their jobs. Again, as the day before, I found myself drawn to Carol. I was often in her vicinity, stealing glances and listening to the beautiful melody that I have come to know as her voice. At one point, I actually brushed my fingers across her shoulder and could feel her body quiver at my touch. I remember feeling a deep sense of regret for my actions of the night before.

When our meal arrived, I saw Carol bolt from the room, and I was concerned for she hadn't spoken to me all day much less looked at me. After she had been gone for five minutes, I went to the women's room to find her. As I opened the door, I could hear her sniffles and I knew she was crying. I berated myself for causing it again and, at that moment, decided it was time to share my epiphany with her.

I waited until the meeting ended, and when I saw Carol was the first to the door to leave, I spoke out. "Carol, could you give me a minute?"

She stood in front of me. Her eyes seemed to be searching my face, and I wondered what I could say to make things right. I suddenly felt vulnerable, fearing that if I revealed myself I'd be giving her the upper hand, and I couldn't allow that. Unable to stop myself, the old Jac surfaced, and with all the bravado I could muster, I asked, "What is your problem?" She intentionally moved back to create distance between us, which surprised me. Her cold reply surprised me. After all, I was Jac, no one ever turns me down, and Carol would be no different. Was I ever wrong. She walked out on me.

Despite my momentary lapse back to the old Jac, I did hear her words and they broke my heart. She was hurting because of me. My rejection of her was destroying the sweet, wonderful woman who gave my soul life. She had to know. Carol needed to understand why I was acting the way I was. I needed to make it all better and vowed to do just that the next day.

✝

The group was gathered, but one was missing. Carol. Repeated calls to her room went unanswered, and I became terrified something had happened to her. I left the group and raced in my car to the hotel. Once in front of her door, I pounded loudly until I heard a stirring in the room. When she finally opened the door, what I saw overwhelmed me. There she was all warm and sleepy; her blonde hair was spiky as if Jacques, the nighttime hairdresser, had paid her a visit. And, much to my surprise and pleasure, she was completely naked.

"Are you okay?" I asked, trying hard not to stare at her nipples that were definitely reacting to the change in temperature.

She seemed to suddenly realize why I was there and spun around losing her balance. I caught her and found myself drowning in the need and want of her. Our kisses at first were soft then progressed to hot and intense. The feel of her bare back under my fingertips only ignited my desire more, and I knew that soon there would be no turning back.

When our long, intense kiss ended, she pleaded with me to make love to her. Oh, I wanted nothing more. How easy it would have been to lose myself in her forever. Although I could not let that happen, I was reluctant to let her go. I couldn't really blame her for pushing away from me or berating my intentions. The anger on her face was evident, but for me the hurt was more palpable. I knew it was because of me.

Once again, I decided I needed to let her know the truth. "Carol, we need to talk. Will you have dinner with me tonight? I promise to answer all your questions."

Her reaction was understandable. "Questions, I don't have any, Jac. You've made your feelings perfectly clear. There is no need for explanations or to have dinner." The sight of her tears ripped at my heart. "Look at this," she says pointing to the liquid streaming down her cheeks, "I don't cry for anyone, nor do I beg. You caused this!"

I see that her anger is turning into rage. "I don't know what you want from me, nor do I care anymore. I won't let that happen again for it hurts too much." She turned away from me. "I need to get ready. I will be there within the hour. You can show yourself out."

I, of course, waited to take her to the meeting. The cold inside the car was as palpable as the words left unsaid. Once we were inside and at the meeting, I couldn't erase her face and the pain I had inflicted upon it. All I wanted to do was take her in my arms and make it all better yet to do that would only make things worse.

When we broke for lunch, I saw her approaching me. I was eager to end my conversation with Ron and speak with her. Our eyes made contact, but Ron drew me back into the discussion with him. Suddenly, I heard the crashing of a chair and looked to see Carol gazing at me all flustered. I couldn't help but smile, for in that instant she was so very adorable.

For me, all hope had been lost that I would ever get the chance to speak privately with Carol until that moment when she was inching toward me. When I heard her speak, "What time are you picking me up for dinner? I have to warn you ahead of time, I'm not a cheap date." My mind and body were on fire, for I knew that I would ignore all else and give in to the desire raging in my body and soul.

✝

I took her to a small, out of the way restaurant that had been a favorite of mine for years. Never before had I brought anyone there, for it was my special place when I just wanted to have a good meal without the difficulty of another person there. But, Carol was not a complication. I welcomed the opportunity to share this private place with her.

The meal was superb, as always, and our conversation was light and casual. It was over dessert that she said, "You know, Jac, it is like I have always known you."

I knew the moment had come to tell her everything, even if that niggling little voice kept cautioning me. "Remember when I told you I had seen you at a conference several years ago?" I said to her.

"Yes."

"Well, when I opened the door the first thing I heard was your voice and that is what drew me in. I remember your words, 'If we ignore what has happened in the past, we never will recognize what is familiar about now...' Something deep inside me was crying out to listen to the beautiful music that your voice elicited in me. I had heard you before deep in a memory...perhaps a dream, but I knew you. Then, when I saw your face, my heart rejoiced for it knew I had found what I had been searching for all my life."

I looked into her eyes, seeing what I believed was a depth of love, and the realization that I was the object of that love shocked me. I was certain that no one had ever loved me with such depth and intensity before. The connection, the desire, and the love were undeniable, and it was time to act upon those feelings. "I think it is time we go back to your room," I said, as the fire burned hot inside my soul.

I knew that there would be no excuses, no turning away. We would be one and not only would she be mine, but I would be hers. The rightness of it all seemed so clear to me, yet the voice deep in my soul protested and became louder and more insistent. By the time we reached the hotel, I understood what the voice was telling me. *Do this now and be forever sentenced to repeat this for all time.* Somehow, I knew that this was our last chance to get it right. If I acted on my emotions, our souls would never join as one. You see, I had no other choice for her words were clear and unmistakable. *"If we ignore what has happened in the past, we never will recognize what is familiar about now..."*

We stepped into her room, and I kissed her before pulling away. "Carol, you know how we said we knew each other?" I asked softly.

"Yes."

"I believe that we have met in many lifetimes and keep repeating the same mistake. I want you, but I can't have you...not now anyway. You belong to another, and I must not interfere."

"You're unbelievable." She steps away from me. "I can't believe I keep falling for your lines of excuses. Well, not anymore. Please leave."

"It is not an excuse, Carol. If we do this now, it will affect all our future lives. Please, believe me." I couldn't believe that I was begging. I never do that.

"Just go." She turned her back on me but not before I saw the tears forming in her eyes.

"I'm sorry." I went to the door and, with my hand on the knob, I said, "I'm sorry," before I left.

†

When I arrived at her hotel room the next day, I really wasn't surprised that she wasn't there. I couldn't blame her, for I had hurt her deeply without any real explanation of why. What sane person would believe what I said? Even I had a hard time believing it, but in my soul I knew it to be true. She deserved better and she would never know that what I did was out of love.

When I got back to my office, I wrote her a letter trying desperately to explain what I was feeling and why things had turned out as they had. I had a courier service deliver it to her that day. Over that weekend, I found myself picking up the phone and dialing her number, only to hang up before it connected. She had to understand that I loved her enough to let her go.

When my phone rang on Monday, I was elated to hear her voice. From that point forward, we forged a wonderful bond based on a deep and abiding love. Although we never met in person again, we had a rich and full friendship filled with long daily phone calls and letters. Often, we would spend our entire lunch times just talking and laughing in a remarkably easy and familiar way. With the end of our conversations we would both say, "I love you always and forever." It was our bond that we sealed each time before the call ended.

Chapter Twelve

Today, I will see her for the first time in almost a year. Deep inside me, I long to touch her and feel her presence. I am to present her with an award for her outstanding achievement in developing a new structure of social services. I am glad her husband, Mike, is coming with her, for it will take some of the sexual tension we will feel away. She will be arriving any moment now, and I need to get down to the front of the auditorium.

My mind drifts back to our last conversation when she told me that her daughter Kathleen had just called her and told her that she would be a grandmother. I heard such joy in Carol's voice as she spoke of what her daughter having her grandchild meant to her. "Jac, it means that I will continue," she told me. That simple statement gave me hope that the decision I'd made was the right one.

I smile and rise from my seat and begin walking toward the crowd gathered in the auditorium. As always, I work the crowd just like a seasoned politician, and I wonder if my performance will win me a Social Services Oscar. I smile and shake hands while taking a moment to speak to everyone I meet. Over the years, I have developed a system for remembering people's names, even if I've only met them once, and that is to my advantage on this day.

All the while, my eyes are scanning the auditorium, searching for the one person that will make me complete again. Carol has not arrived yet and apprehension fills me. *She should have been here by now.* Suddenly, I can feel it. Disbelief and horror fills my soul. While standing there among the crowd of people, I begin to shake before letting out a wail of pain. I can see people turn toward me. It isn't long before a circle of onlookers gape at me. I am standing with my arms encircling my body desperately holding it to keep myself from collapsing.

"What's happening? Is she all right? Isn't that Dr. Reinhart? Is she having a seizure or a heart attack? Someone should call 911," the crowd around me whispers loudly.

A woman pushes through the crowd and approaches me before putting an arm around me. I look at her, but I don't seem to recognize who she is. "It's okay, Jac, I've got you," she whispers in my ear. I know that I am incoherent as my mind fills with unbelievable grief.

Whoever the woman is, she leads me to the back of the auditorium where she sits me down. I begin to rock as sobs well up in me and explode. The woman wraps an arm around me and holds me tight. "I've got you, Jac. Everything will be okay."

How can everything be okay? My world is collapsing and my heart and soul are screaming. My other half is lost to me and I am alone.

I hear a woman in the front of the immense room tap on a microphone, "May I have your attention please?" Her voice is low and serious and I know what she is going to say. I try to shut it out but I cannot. "Our honoree and guest speaker, Carol Barngate, has been in an accident on her way here and is in the hospital. Please join me in a moment of prayer for her speedy recovery."

The arm around me tightens and I look to see who it is. Evelyn Delarosa, Carol's friend and coworker is holding me. "She's gone," I whisper before another sob wracks my body.

"No, they just said she is at the hospital and they are treating her."

I can feel my head shaking. "She's gone," I repeat.

"You don't know that, Jac."

"But I do." I put my hand over my heart. "I know it in here." My body begins to shiver with the truth of my words.

Evelyn kisses the top of my head. "It can't be. I was just speaking with her less than a half hour ago. She was so excited and told me she was looking forward to seeing you again. She can't be gone."

Her words cut deep into my heart. Carol called me when her plane arrived in Dallas. Her words were full of promise. *I'll be seeing you in less than an hour and, once again, we will be together. I'll call you when I'm settled.* Did I miss her call? I fumble for my phone and see a missed call and a voice mail. With trembling fingers, I press play.

"Hi, I guess you are busy getting ready. We will be leaving soon and I can't wait. Seeing you again in person is a moment I've waited for ever since I saw you last. Jac, I have so much I want to say. See you soon."

"Oh, God, no. Don't let it be." I melt into Evelyn's arms and darkness fills my heart and soul.

†

It has been twenty-six years to the day since I lost Carol. The love of my life is gone and, for me, life has become nothing more than going through the motions of living day to day without really living. Fifteen years ago, I left government work and began a private company with the primary focus on battered and abused woman and children. The credo of my company incorporates all of Carol's ideas and methods as a tribute to her memory. I have become so entrenched in my work that there are moments I actually don't think about her, but those instances are rare.

Every day since her passing, I curse myself for listening to some absurd idea that I needed to break the cycle. She is gone from me, and I never knew the complete joy of being with her. Why was I so stupid? Me, 'Jac the invincible,' listening to some mystical babble that left me with nothing more than a shell of a life. For the most part, I live my life robotically, only letting my sorrow show in the darkness of the early morning when sleep eludes me.

I think sometimes that all the medication I am taking for the cancer is what makes my dreams about Carol so vivid and real. My time is nearing its end, and I welcome the finality of it. I close my eyes and, as sleep takes me, I remember it all again.

The cemetery where her body lays brings me little comfort, but I travel there in my dreams anyway. I can see myself reading the words as I stand at the granite marker before squatting down and tracing the name Carol Elizabeth Barngate with my fingers. My heart is heavy with longing and bereavement. It is the anniversary of our first meeting, and I am visiting the cemetery just as I always do, placing a white rose on her headstone.

In the dream, I can feel the tears flowing down my cheeks just as they always have. This time though, a chill is seeping into my body and I look up and frown. A mist is creeping along the ground, enveloping all the grave stones. Soon it is so thick that I cannot see. I stand and stumble among the garden of stones, feeling lost and alone but unafraid. My feet seem to have a mind of their own as they carry me through the mist.

I am sitting in a clearing near a peaceful lake. The sun is rising, and the fire of the night before is but warm embers. I clutch a large blanket around my shoulders to ward off the early morning chill. The dreams of the night before still haunt me, as they do every time I awaken.

The morning mist is still rising, and the air is sweet with the perfume of a spring morning. I am waiting, just as I have for a very long time.

In the distance, out of the mist, comes a vision, and I instantly know my wait is over and my heart fills with never ending joy and peace.

I arise and walk toward the apparition coming to me until our eyes meet. "I have been waiting for you," I say softly.

The vision reaches out and takes my hand before slowly lifting it to her lips, reverently. Lightly, she places a single kiss on each finger. "I came as soon as I could," she whispers.

"I knew you would come."

"The spell has been broken...we will be together forever and this time we will get it right."

I take her hand and we walk through the mist into a new day.

With a start, I sit up in my bed. The dream, just as it has been every night for the last month, seems so real that I am sure I can smell the sweetness of the air. I close my eyes, and suddenly Carol's voice sings in my ears. "We will be together soon, my love." I know that her words are true. I close my eyes and let sleep take me again.

Chapter Thirteen

Livvy—Anamchara

The sound of running water wakes me from a blissful sleep. Opening my eyes, I stare at the white swirled ceiling of a suite in the Hotel Monaco in Washington DC. My body is naked, and I am sure I still feel kisses lingering every-where as the taste and smell of her fills my senses. Never in my wildest imaginations could I believe anything or anyone could move me to such a passionate encounter. Yet, here I am, pulling back the soft, white sheet, letting my bare feet touch the richly carpeted floor, walking toward the bath-room, and opening the door. I can't help myself. I want—no need—to feel her luscious body next to mine again.

A feeling of déjà vu sweeps over me and I shiver at its power. How is this possible? How did I get to this place?

†

My life, living in a suburb of Los Angeles, has always been happy. I've just finished getting a master's degree in social justice and accepted a job at a social work consortium of researchers, planners, and policy makers located in Virginia. I did not intend to move from California, but for some reason, the position attracted me and I applied for the job. I got it.

As the time draws near to make the move, the question becomes; do I really want to leave all that I've ever known to follow something that was telling me instinctually to go? In my heart, I know the answer—something in Virginia is beckoning me, and I have no other choice but to follow.

I'm ensconced in my bedroom, going through all the treasures of my twenty-six-year lifetime, trying to figure out what I need to take with me. Although the room has had new paint over the years, it still reflects a girl's bedroom. There is a white, four-poster bed with a purple ruffle skirt and a matching bedspread. My mother insisted the room remain the same while I was away at college. Looking around now, I begrudgingly admit to myself that I'll miss the room.

There are so many memories that I've held on to and they overwhelm me. I'm wondering exactly why I still have a doll from when I was two, when I hear a light tap on the doorframe. I look up and see my mother with her arms folded, leaning against the doorjamb of my bedroom.

"Whatcha doin'?"

"Taking a trip down memory lane." I hold up the doll. "Why do I still have her?"

Mom laughs. "Good question. She's so damn ugly I'm surprised you still have her. Find anything else interesting?

I shrug and look away. "So many memories."

"Hey, what's going on? Are you worried about the move?"

"Yeah, a little. I'm leaving the only home I've known to fly across the country to live in a strange place where I don't know anyone. I must be crazy."

Mom comes in and sits next to me on my bed. "It's a great career opportunity, and if you get there and don't like it you always have a home here."

"I know all that. It's just...oh, I don't know."

"Come on and show me what you found that's made you so pensive."

I hold up a small notebook. "Remember when I was in the eleventh grade, I had a project on genealogy?"

Mom gives me a small smile then looks away. "Eleventh grade? That was, what, ten years ago? What else have you found?" She starts sorting through the box on the purple bedspread, but I put my hand on hers and stop her.

"I know you remember. I can see it on your face. Remember, we had that big fight when I asked about my grandmother." She still won't look at me. "You know who I'm talking about, don't you? You named me after her yet only call me by my middle name. Why?"

"Olivia was your dad's mother's name, and he started calling you *Livvy* when you were born."

I grab her hand and squeeze it. "That's no reason for not telling me about your mother."

"Livvy, I can't go there." I see her eyes; they are brimming with tears and she closes them, causing a small rivulet to roll down her cheek.

"Why? Did she kill someone? Was she a serial killer? You and Uncle Mike turned out pretty good, so she couldn't have been a horrible mother." I squeeze the hand I am still holding. "I never met her, and I want to know about her. Please, tell me."

"Not only do you look exactly like her, you're just as tenacious." She let out a small laugh. "That's why you will be so good at your new job."

"Mom, you're deflecting. Please, tell me."

She gets off the bed and walks over to the door. "I'll be right back." She leaves my room and I wait.

I can hear her rummaging through what sounds like a drawer. When she returns, she hands me a picture.

I look at it and swallow hard. It is as if I am looking in a mirror. "Does my looking like her make you sad?"

"No, sweetheart. You remind me each day of her. It is sometimes like she is here with me." She shrugs. "I know it's you in case you were wondering."

"Is that why you won't tell me about her? You think I might be upset?"

In those few words, she's given me more information about my grandmother than she ever has. Still, I don't understand her reticence in not telling me about her over the years.

"No. In its own way, it is a comfort and makes me remember the good times."

"The bad times must have been horrible if you can't even speak about her. Please, tell me."

For what seems like a long moment, she remains silent. When she finally speaks, it is in a soft reflective voice. "I remember the last time I talked to her." She shakes her head and has a rueful look on her face. "I was telling her that I was pregnant with you. There was such joy in her voice, and I was glad I could be the one to put it there."

I watch as a tender smile crosses her face.

"She told me I was having a girl. I laughed since the doctor told us you were a boy. I didn't have the heart to tell her that news. You see, in that last year of her life, she had changed. She became withdrawn and there was a sadness about her that neither my dad nor I understood. I was so glad to hear the smile in her voice that there was no way I was going to tell her I was having a boy."

"Surprise. I'm a girl." I held my arms out. "She must have known somehow."

"I always thought it was a mother's intuition."

"I know that your parents were in a car accident. What happened?"

"She was being honored for outstanding achievement—I don't really remember what it was for—but I know it was a big deal and I think a national recognition. They had flown to Dallas for the presentation. On their way to the meeting, it was raining and a motorcycle slid on the wet pavement, causing a chain reaction. A semi landed on top of the rental they were driving. Mercifully, they both died instantly." Tears rolled down her cheek.

"I had no idea. It must have been devastating for you." I get off my bed and go to her, wrapping her in my arms.

"It was. After the funeral, I went back to California and I began spotting. The doctor told me that I had to be very careful and restricted my travel so I never was able to say good-bye properly. I never visited their home—the house where I grew up—to touch and remember everything. Uncle Mike's family was growing, and they had been looking for a new home, so it was logical that they move into Mom and Dad's."

"Do you resent him for that?"

"At times." She steps out of the embrace, and I watch as she swipes at her tears with her shirt sleeve. "Mostly, I've just tried to put it out of my mind. It was what it was and there was no sense in stewing over it. Nothing I could do would change it. I needed to take care of myself so I could deliver a healthy baby. By the time I did visit my parent's home, everything was changed."

"Is that why you wouldn't talk to me about her?" I'm still puzzled.

She looks at me and shakes her head. "No. There's more to it than that."

"Please, tell me." I take her by the hand and lead her to the bed where we sit down.

"A year later, Mike was cleaning out the garage and found a box of her things and sent it to me along with several other boxes that belonged to her. He thought I might like to have the mementos. One of the boxes contained the things from her office at work. I was astounded by the number of awards she'd received, and I realized just how little I knew about her outside of being mom." I hear her take in a deep breath and watch as the expression on her face becomes one of deep sadness and something else that I can't quite decipher. I wait until she looks at me and sighs. "I found a small metal box that had letters and a journal in it."

"Did you read what was there?"

"I thought it would give me insight into her life at work. Boy was I wrong. There was a stack of letters tied together with a piece of blue ribbon, and I made the mistake of reading the first letter. After that, I put it all away for that letter told me everything. I knew why she had suddenly become sad. She was having an affair with a coworker."

I could feel my forehead wrinkle. "Are you sure?"

"Yes. It was all there in the letter I read. The other person was professing her undying love for my mother."

"Her?"

"Yes. Jac was her name."

"So you just wrote your mother out of your life because she was a lesbian?" I frown. "Wow. I had no idea. You must have really been disappointed when I came out to you." I let go of her hand and move away.

"No. God, no, Livvy. That's not true."

116

There is an apology in her expression and I shrug, wondering how sincere she is. "So what...she didn't live up to who you thought she was so you wrote her off?"

"Yes, essentially, I guess that is what I did." She looks at me. "Not my proudest moment, but to my way of thinking she betrayed my dad, Mike, and me."

"How did she betray you? Her loving a woman had nothing to do with you." I was finding it difficult to contain *my* disappointment in her. I always thought my mom didn't have a problem with my being a lesbian. Suddenly, I am not so sure.

Mom rubs her chin and lets out a sigh. "She didn't betray me...my dad was the one she hurt the most."

"Did he know what was going on?"

"I don't know. I know he was worried about her."

"So you judged her and wrote her off without knowing all the facts?" I was having a hard time understanding my mother's position. "The mother I know never would turn her back on someone like that. Especially considering she is gone and isn't here to defend herself."

"Obviously, you don't know me as well as you think you do." My mom begins to shake, and I pull her close and hold her as her tears fall. After a while, she looks up at me.

"A year later, I finally tracked down that woman and told her what I thought of her. She, of course, denied anything happened. I had the evidence, called her a liar, and told her to stop putting the damned white rose on her grave. That was all before slapping her in the face. A week later, she sent me a letter—I shredded it without opening it."

I look at her, wondering how I could have missed this side of her. "I've never known you to be so judgmental. All my life, you've told me to look at all sides and never jump to conclusions. Why did you do that to your mother of all people?"

"I was hurt and angry with her. Mom was always my hero."

"And you found she was just like the rest of us…flawed with feet of clay."

She looks away. "I suppose so."

"Do you still have the letters and the journal?"

"Yes. Even though I despised what she'd done, I couldn't let that last tangible part of her go. Strange isn't it?"

"She was your mother and you still loved her."

"At the time I didn't."

"Yes, you probably did love her, and that is what made it worse."

A genuine smile curves her lips. "When did you get to be so wise?"

"I had a good teacher." I hug her and kiss her cheek. "Will you let me read them?"

She pulls away and her eyes search my face. "Why would you want to do that?"

"Because she is a part of me and her blood runs through me. I want to know her too."

Mom sighs and then gets up. "Okay, I'll get them for you." She begins to leave then stops. "Livvy, I don't care who you love. That has never been an issue."

I smile and nod at her and say, "Okay," even though I'm not as sure of that as I once was.

†

The next morning, after reading the journal and letters late into the night, I drag myself down the stairs to the kitchen. Mom is sitting at the table drinking coffee and looking out the patio door.

"You look like you didn't sleep much either." I get a cup out of the cupboard and pour myself a coffee. Taking a sip, I sit across from Mom.

"I saw your light on and knew you were reading that damned journal."

I close my eyes as the caffeine enters my body. "You should have read more than just that one letter. It would have saved you all the years of resentment you had toward her."

"I read all I needed to."

I can tell by her tone that she is on edge and probably regrets letting me read the journal. "If you read further you would have discovered that they were never intimate. They were in love and very close, but they were never lovers."

"I don't believe that. I know what I read."

"Mom, Jac wrote to your mom and told her that this wasn't their lifetime and that it wasn't fair to Grandad, Uncle Mike, or you."

She glares at me. "No, that can't be."

"I figured you'd say that." I take the letter out of my pocket and gave it to her. As she reads, I watch the play of emotions on her face. At first, her jaw is set in what looks like anger and then, as her eyes run across the words, her face begins to soften. Finally, tears roll down her cheeks.

"All those years I resented her and what I thought she'd done to our family. There is no other word for it...I detested that Jac woman with every fiber of my body." She puts her hand over her mouth and sobs. "I was so horrible to her."

"Do you remember how to contact her?"

Mom shakes her head. "No, I destroyed everything I had."

"Any idea what her last name is?"

"All I remember is that her first name was Jacqueline."

"What did she look like?"

A smile creeps across her lips. "I must say that your grandmother had excellent taste in women. I remember when I first saw her thinking that she surely didn't look like what I thought she would."

"Why?"

"She was probably in her mid-forties, had a commanding stature, and was gorgeous. What I saw certainly didn't fit my preconceived notion of her. But, I didn't let that dissuade me for as far as I was concerned she was a predator that had corrupted my mother."

"But, she wasn't. From what I read, she was an honorable woman who loved Grandma Carol deeply and wanted to do the right thing by her family." I put my arm around her shoulders. "From what I read, Grandma was having some difficulties at work, and Jac sent her a locket that she had specially made for her. She wrote that if she was ever in doubt about anything to hold it between her fingers and she'd know what to do."

"That sounds weird."

"According to your mom, it worked."

She looks suitably distraught by the news. "I always wondered where that necklace came from. Dad didn't give it to her, so I assumed she'd bought it for herself."

"It seems that there was more to Jac than you gave her credit for."

Mom looks up at me with tears still in her eyes. "I always stressed for you to look at all the facts before drawing a conclusion, and I didn't heed my own advice. I should have read it all, but I let my emotions get in the way with a knee jerk reaction." She looks out the patio door and sighs. "It is now something I will always regret."

"Where did you meet her?"

"We didn't have all the information, back then, that the internet provides today. I figured she went to the funeral and asked Mike to look at the guest book to see if there was someone with the first name of Jac or Jacqueline, and he found her name. From there I was able to track her to the symposium that my parents were going to when they died."

"Do you remember anything about what she was doing there?"

Mom scrunches her forehead. "She had some role, but I can't remember what it was."

"It's too bad you don't remember more about her. I would have liked to speak with her. I wish I was an investigator so I could find the elusive Jac." I give her a grin.

"Why on earth would you want to do that?"

"Mom, she saw a side of your mother, my grandmother, that you never got to see."

I watch my mom's jaw work. "I resented the woman. She was a stranger who invaded our family's lives." She shakes her head. "I appreciate you telling me what you've found about this Jac person, but I cannot forgive her as easily as you seem to have."

"Mom, it isn't about forgiveness. It's about understanding who your mother was and how she conducted her life. She remained loyal to her family, despite how she felt about Jac. That must count for something."

Mom's tears flow freely, and it isn't long before she becomes inconsolable.

I cradle her in my arms until her cries subside into short sobs.

Her watery eyes fix on me. "I know you have to, but I don't want you to go."

I put my hand over my heart. "Mom, something in here is telling me this is the right job for me. As soon as I saw the posting it called to me, and I have to find out what it is."

"I understand, but I still don't have to like it."

I know the truth behind her words, but I also know that something is missing from my life and until I figure it out, I will always be incomplete.

Chapter Fourteen

The days flew by. I said good-bye to all my friends. It was with sadness laced with a healthy dose of anticipation that I went to bed the night before we were to leave. The fact that I slept soundly is a surprise to me as I bound out of bed and into the shower. This will be my last breakfast in California, and I make my way down the stairs and into the kitchen.

Mom is standing at the stove. "Dad is outside checking everything. Can you go tell him breakfast is ready?"

"Yep." I go outside and see my dad checking the tire pressure. "Hey, breakfast is ready."

He comes over to me and engulfs me in a hug. "You ready for this?"

"Yes and no, if that makes any sense."

He grins. "When your mother and I first came to California, I think she cried every day for two weeks. She was homesick and called her mom every day. One day, she found a friend at a gym she was going to and after that, the tears stopped." He hugs me again. "It'll all work out, I promise."

"I'll hold you to that." I kiss his cheek. "Let's eat so we can get on the road."

†

With a U-Haul tracking behind my Prius, the road flies by. I'm glad my mom and dad are going with me. Even though it is prolonging our eventual good-bye, I am grateful to have the time with them. With three people driving and pushing it, we could make the journey in four days but decide to make it a pleasure trip and do some sightseeing along the way.

The first day we drive almost eight hours to Bryce Canyon National Park where we spend the night. The next day we visit the spectacular canyon, and Monday we drive to Colorado and spend the night in Rocky Mountain National Park, awe inspiring to say the least. I even see my first moose. Our journey continues across the States, stopping in St. Louis and going up in the Arch. In Pittsburg, we visit the wonderful Carnegie Museum of Natural History before heading out on the final leg to Reston, Virginia and the apartment I've sublet for the next six months.

Through a sudden downburst of rain, I see a sign that reads *Reston 15 miles* and sigh. "We're almost there. My butt feels like it is glued to the seat."

"Want to pull over? I'll drive," my dad says.

"No, I'm good. Besides, if we stop and get out we'll get soaked."

"You can stop on the shoulder of the overpass ahead. Won't get wet."

I laugh. "But we will get the spray from passing cars. I'm good."

"Hopefully the rain will have stopped by the time we get to your apartment," Mom says from the back seat. "I'll check out the radar on my phone."

"What's our plan of attack?" Dad looks over at me.

"Unpack the trailer, go to the market, and have a nice dinner before collapsing into bed."

"The rain should be ending anytime now." Mom leans over the seat to show Dad the radar map on her phone. "Why don't I go to the market while you and Dad unload? Thank goodness, the apartment is on the first floor. I can't imagine what it would be like to climb stairs with all your boxes."

"Mom, there *is* an elevator, but I'm glad to be on the ground floor. I'm excited for you guys to see the place. I think you'll approve."

†

It's taken us three days, but we finally have everything arranged, the pantry filled, and the refrigerator stocked with perishables. Standing by Mom, I survey the room in front of me. Even though the furniture isn't mine, the place definitely reflects me now that my things are in place. I look at the bookcase that has pictures of my family and see the one of my grandmother that Mom insisted I take. It is still a touchy subject for her, but she is making an effort. I feel her arm go around my shoulders.

"It looks like we have everything arranged. Can you think of anything else we need to do before we leave tomorrow?" Mom asks. "Wait, I think it needs something more."

Puzzled by her words I look at her. "What? I thought we emptied all the boxes."

She holds out a gift bag and hands it to me. "I made this for you."

I look inside and see the afghan she's been crocheting for the last three months. "Mom, it's beautiful. Thank you." I turn and hug her close.

"Whenever you are feeling lonely or afraid just wrap yourself up in it and you will feel my love embracing you."

"Oh, Mom." I can't help the tears that begin to fall.

"No tears, sweetie, this is a new start to your life. Embrace it and be happy."

"If you and Dad hadn't been here, I'd be still knee deep in stuff for months to come." I hug her close. "I'm going to miss you, Mom."

Mom looks away, and I know she is struggling not to cry.

"I have a plane ticket to come home in a month." My words catch in my throat as the reality of the moment hits me. They will leave, and I will be alone.

"I know, darling." She rests her head on my shoulder. "You'll do fine here I just know it."

"I'm glad your flight doesn't leave until the afternoon. It'll give me more time with you and Dad."

"Hey, anyone interested in sushi? I found a little place not far from here," Dad says, as he comes in the door.

I have to laugh, for my dad's enthusiasm is contagious. "Let me get a quick shower, and I'll be ready to go."

"Make it quick. My stomach has been rumbling ever since I went into the place and had a sample. It was delicious."

"I won't be long." I rush toward the bathroom, hoping that neither Mom nor Dad can see the tears in my eyes. I want to cling to them for as long as I can. Logically, I know that living on my own is long overdue, but that doesn't help dissolve the ache in my heart at the thought.

†

Sunday afternoon, I return from the airport to my empty apartment and slump down on the couch with tears soaking my cheeks. This is the first time in my life that family is not somewhere near where I live. Until now, I haven't considered that I was rash in deciding to move across the country. The ache in my heart is acute, but I know I must make the best of it for now.

"I can always go home."

Tomorrow I start working at the Anamchara—pronounced ann-am kara—Institute an on-going social services consortium. When I first heard the name, I thought it was strange. After I looked up the meaning—the Irish word for soulmate—I thought it even weirder, since the primary mission of the institute is brainstorming and devising plans for the care of battered and abused women and children. Nevertheless, for reasons I still don't understand, I feel compelled to work there. I met two of the other analysts when I was there for orientation a month ago, so I have a frame of reference when I get there.

They seemed nice enough. One of them, Briana O'Hara, took me out for dinner and I had a nice time. She told me when I moved here we'd get together and she'd take me around to see the sights.

"Where did I put her phone number?" I rummage through my briefcase and finally come up with Briana's number. I debate for all of a minute as whether to call her or not. I am lonely and don't want to spend the rest of the day alone. Even though it is already close to five o'clock and tomorrow is a workday, I pull out my cell and dial her number.

"Hello."

"Briana?"

"Yes, who is this?"

"It's Livvy Michelson. I'm the new analyst at the institute. We met about a month ago…we went out to dinner."
God, I'm rambling. I never ramble.

"Yes, of course, Livvy. Call me Bri, most everyone does."

"Okay, Bri, it is."

"Are you all settled in?"

"Yes, thankfully, my parents came with me and helped me get things in order."

"Nothing sucks more than trying to do that alone. If you still have more to do let me know and I'll round up a crew."

"Isn't that the truth. Thanks for the offer and I just might take you up on it." I laugh. Bri seems like a person that I'd like to be friends with, in and out of work. "I'm sorry I didn't call sooner, but I just got back from taking my folks to the airport. Are you free for dinner?"

"Oh, Livvy, I'm sorry I can't. I'm at my parent's house getting ready for a big family dinner."

"Darn. I guess I left it too long. We can do it another time. Sorry to bother you. I'll see you tomorrow."

"No bother. I'll see you tomorrow then. Bye, Livvy. I'm glad you will be joining us. We have a great team."

"It seems that way. Bye." I know I sound like a petulant child as I end the call. I look around the room, wondering what to do now. I think about my parents. After ten days of being in a car together then here unpacking, I am secretly glad that I have some time alone to breathe. In my heart, I know that if they came through the door I'd welcome them warmly. Alone is something I need to get used to doing.

I pick up a book of poetry by Sara Teasdale and begin reading some of my favorite poems. Restless, I don't get very far. I put the book down and go into the kitchen to make myself something to eat. Although I have a large assortment of things to choose from, I find nothing appealing. My eyes glance at the freezer section and I smile. "Oh, I'm sure that the tub of chocolate-chocolate chunk ice cream is calling my name."

Just as I settle on the couch with spoon and ice cream in hand, my phone rings. I smile. "Did you get there?"

"Yes, darling. We are safe, sound, and on our way to Providence."

"I'm glad. You know if you want you can come back this way before going back home."

"You're going to be fine, and I will call you every day."

"Oh, Mom, sometimes I wonder if I'm doing the right thing, but mostly I'm excited and nervous at the same time."

"Darling, remember when you first went to UCLA you called me every day for two months, and then you made friends and those calls became a few times a week. You're going on a great adventure, embrace it and, most of all, have fun."

"I'm so stoked to be going." I hear myself sigh with happiness and laugh. "But why did I have to go so far away?"

Mom laughs too. "I bet that in less than a month you'll be settled in and having the time of your life. Remember to make the most of every opportunity." I hear her chuckle. "Even the lemons that sometimes show up."

"I will. Thanks, Mom. I can always count on you to put things in perspective, especially with that tired old lemon comment. Is Dad there?"

"No. He and Mike went to pick up a pizza."

"They went to Vinny's, didn't they?"

"Of course, is there any other pizza place?"

"No." I could feel my body trembling. "I can taste their tomato pie. Damn, I should have gone with you just for that." I laugh.

"I'll see if we can send you one, although it might be a bit soggy when it gets there."

"Yuck, I think I'll pass."

"Good idea. Do you want me to have Dad call you when he gets back?"

"No, I'll call him tomorrow. Right now, I have to eat some ice cream that's melting. After that, I think I'll go to bed. It's been long day and I'm exhausted."

"An intense few weeks is more like it."

I chuckle. "I think you are right."

"Good luck tomorrow. Call me when you get home and tell me how your first day went."

"I will." I feel trepidation fill my heart.

"Good night. Sweet dreams."

"Good night, Mom."

After ending the call, I take a bite of the ice cream and look around the room. My eyes rest on the box that contains my grandmother's correspondence with Jac. I did a search for Jac while in California and came up empty.

Even with all the information available on the internet, twenty plus years have passed and information about Jac is elusive. I was able to locate information on the symposium, only to find that there were twenty-five hundred attendees, including one hundred women with the name of Jacqueline. Seventy-five of them were in the right age range. I was able to track down fifty of those, leaving the remaining twenty-five unaccounted for and thereby ending my search. Maybe, with the resources of the institute I will be able to find out something more.

I pull open my laptop and begin looking again. "I'll find you, Jac. It's just a matter of digging a bit deeper." The next thing I know, I'm looking at the bottom right of the screen and see it is one in the morning. "Damn."

Chapter Fifteen

Thunder had rumbled all night, and when a bolt of lightning made the building shake, my eyes opened. I look at the time on the clock—*five twenty and it's still dark.* "Damn."

If I stay in bed, I know that I won't sleep. I drag myself out of bed with my eyes feeling like they have sand in them. I make my way to the kitchen, yawning the entire time. The coffeepot, set to go on at seven, hasn't started brewing yet and I let out a low growl. After punching a few buttons, I lean against the counter doing a few stretches while contemplating the day ahead.

When I visited the institute a month earlier, everyone was dressed in business casual. Back home, during the summer, I was a gofer in my dad's law office and I always wore a suit—even on Fridays. For this new job, I picked out a pair of black slacks and a cream-colored shell to go under a lightweight, grey sweater. Stodgy, I know, but until I have a better handle on the dress code, I'm going to play it safe.

"Finally." The coffee finishes brewing and I pour myself a cup. After a quick swallow, I take the cup and head back to my bedroom. Knowing that I have extra time, I decide to take a bath. I am feeling keyed-up and need to relax.

By seven thirty, I am out of the tub and re-ironing my clothes. No way do I want to show up with wrinkles. When I open the underwear drawer, I see a small box with a folded note under it, resting on top of my panties. I lift the box and open it. I see a necklace that has one gold circle surrounding four entwined gold hearts. With trembling fingers, I pick up the note.

Livvy, this is the necklace I'm sure that Jac gave to my mother. I want you to have it as a memory of your grandmother.
Love, Mom

"It's a start toward healing, Mom." I take the necklace out of the box and hold it in my palm as feelings of grief fill me. I wonder if it is because I miss my family, but my heart tells me there is so much more. Once I put it on, the sadness I was feeling changes to happiness. *That's odd.*

The chime of a phone alarm tells me I need to be at work in an hour and takes me out of the moment. I fold the note and place it and the box on the dresser, before gathering my bra and panties and starting to dress.

✝

With a slight bit of trepidation, I put the lanyard with my badge around my neck, before getting out of my car and walking toward my new life. The guard inside the lobby is a wizened man with snow-white hair and a ruddy complexion.

"Good morning. You must be the new hire," he says with a friendly smile. "I've been expecting you."

I hold out my hand. "Livvy Michelson."

He takes my hand and gives it a shake. "I'll let Mr. McCrea know you're here. If you'll just take a seat, it won't take long."

Soon, Aldridge McCrea comes striding toward me. "Good morning. Are you all settled in?" Aldridge is a tall man, whose shiny, bald head has light bouncing off it.

"Yes, thank you."

"Follow me. I've asked Briana to join us."

I am glad to hear this, since I have a feeling that Briana and I will become good friends. "Great. Anyone else?"

"No. Briana is our most experienced analyst, and she will be your mentor."

"Lead the way."

†

Bri looks up and smiles when I enter the room. "Good morning and welcome."

I smile at her and move closer, holding out my hand. She is easy on the eyes and someone I might want to get to know better on a personal level. Over the years, I've dated both women and men, finally deciding that I prefer women. If I'm not mistaken, Bri probably would be receptive to having a relationship with a woman.

"I want you two to work as a team," Aldridge says, sliding into the chair at his desk. "There is a new scenario that will need a steady hand and intensive investigation. If the figures and early analysis are any indication, this has the potential of great progress toward understanding the mind-set of abusers." He hands me a folder. "Bri has already started the preliminary work and can update you."

I take the folder, open it, and quickly scan the first page. "Just from what I've read, I see what you mean." I look at Bri. "Looks like we've got our work cut out for us."

"Yes, we do. First, let me show you your office and you can settle in. Did you bring anything with you for the office?"

"I have a couple of boxes in my car."

"I can help you carry them in," Bri says.

Aldridge stands and smiles. "Welcome aboard, Livvy, I'm glad you are joining us. If you need anything at all, there is a list on your desk of all the pertinent phone numbers and employees. Of course, you can always call me or Briana if you have any questions."

"Thank you." I look at Bri. "Shall we go then?"

"Yes."

Once we are out of the office, she says, "I'm really glad we're going to be working together."

"Me too."

†

Over the next month, Bri and I work together with three others, Marvin Welch, Heidi McNamara, and Christine Linamar, solidifying the reports. We also brainstorm ideas that will meet the objective of getting into the minds of abusers. We all work well together, but truth be told, I look forward to seeing only Bri each day.

It doesn't take long for us to form a solid friendship and spend time outside of work together. Once we discover that we both are into history, Bri and I begin visiting both Civil and Revolutionary War sites. The area is ripe with history, and I eagerly accept when she asks if I want to go to York Town, a British stronghold.

Sitting on a bench, Bri has what seems like a faraway look. "Are you okay?" I ask.

Bri nods. "Yeah, I was just remembering the last time I was here."

I sit next to her. It's obvious that whatever happened then is upsetting her. "Want to talk about it?"

She smiles. "I last came here with my best friend, Sara. We actually sat on this bench."

"Does she live nearby?"

"No. She died three years ago."

I wasn't expecting that. I put my arm around her and pull her close. "Do you want to leave?" I say softly.

"No. I'm good. Do you sometimes get strong feelings about a person or a place?"

I think for a moment. "Yeah, I guess I do. Lately a grandmother that I never met is on my mind. Is that what it's like with Sara? I mean, she's in your head."

"In my head and heart." Bri pats my leg. "Hey, there's this great little restaurant, just outside of town. Are you hungry?"

I laugh. "I was hoping you'd say that. I'm starving!"

"I seem to remember you have a hollow pit for a stomach, from the last time we went out. This place makes a fantastic beef stew with homemade biscuits." She stands and holds out her hand. "You game?"

I take her hand and it is warm and inviting. "Absolutely."

Chapter Sixteen

"Hey, Livvy, what are you doing next Saturday?" Bri asks me on a Wednesday during lunch.

"Hmm, let me see." I put my index finger to my temple and tap it. "Nothing. Why?"

"I have tickets to a small gathering for a medium."

"Like a fortune teller?"

Bri laughs nervously. "No. It's not like that at all. She's assisted the police in finding missing persons with a very good record of finding them."

"Oh." I'm puzzled. Bri has always seemed level-headed to me. "Why?"

Bri looks away before fixing me with a gaze from her hazel eyes. "Remember, I told you about my best friend, Sara."

"Yes. She died. Was she in a car accident?"

"No. She had a terrible headache in September and, by January, brain cancer took her from me." I watch as she sucks in a breath. "For the last eighteen months, she keeps popping into my mind at really odd times."

"Like when?" I'm curious to find out more, since I've always sensed sadness in my friend.

"The oddest time is when I'm plucking my eyebrows, and I'm suddenly remembering something about her—like a conversation we had over lunch once or how she had this goofy smile when she was happy. It's as if she is trying to tell me something, but I don't know what that is. Other times, like last week when Christine was complaining of a headache, I wonder if that is Sara telling me to get myself checked out."

"Are you sick?" I ask in alarm.

"No, I'm fine. It's just when someone speaks of a headache I wonder if she is nudging me."

I scratch my cheek trying to get my head around why she wants to see a fortune teller. "And you think this *medium* will help you figure it out?"

"I've been corresponding with her for the last year."

"Who is she? Maybe I've heard of her." I doubt it, but it seems important to Bri, and the least I can do is hear her out.

"Her name is Natasha Gabor."

"Is she Romanian?"

"I don't know. Why are you asking?"

"Gabor is a Romanian last name, that's all." I refrain from telling Bri that Romania has a large gypsy population and maybe that is where the woman got her skills to be a medium.

"Oh." Bri scrunches her face. "I don't know where she is from. She doesn't speak with an accent."

"What exactly can she do for you…and Sara?"

"She sees beyond what ordinary people see. In our correspondence, she said she thinks she can help me find out what Sara is trying to tell me." She shrugs. "I don't know what it is, but I know it is important."

"Why do you need me to go? It sounds like you and this woman already have a connection."

"I don't know her, but I know you. I trust your instincts. I've seen firsthand how you can ferret out the truth of an idea from the smallest of clues." She runs a hand through her hair. "Look, I don't know if this is a scam or not, but I have to give it a try."

"You're absolutely sure that Sara is trying to tell you something?"

"Yes." She holds her hand over her heart. "I feel it in here."

"What will it entail?"

"There is a one on one with Natasha, and a meal is included."

I smile and raise an eyebrow. "If dinner is included, should I consider this a date?"

"Definitely."

"Then I'd love to go with you."

Bri blows out a breath and smiles. "Thank you."

†

With Bri by my side, we step into the small room that oozes an intimate feeling. It certainly isn't what I was expecting. I thought there would be some sort of garish display. Instead, in one corner, a string quartet is playing Borodin's Quartet No. 1, softly. The others standing gathered around the room seem to be an eclectic group of people ranging from my age to an elderly couple. I see four round tables formally set up for a meal, with five chairs situated in a semicircle around each table. In front of that is a smaller table with two chairs on either side.

"It looks like there are only twenty people attending. You must have paid a fortune for the tickets."

"They are complimentary." Bri smiles. "Natasha invited me to join the event with a friend."

"That's amazing." I let my gaze take in the room and recognize that everything is first class. "This can't be cheap." I wonder if she gives everyone free tickets and that is how she draws them in before fleecing them for money. *I won't let that happen to Bri.*

"She should be here soon. I'm anxious to meet her." She squeezes my hand. "I'm glad you're my plus one."

"Me too."

A hush settles over the room and I look, along with everyone else, to the front of the room. A woman with long, black hair seems to be gliding toward us. I appraise her just as I do when I speak with people suspected of beating their kids. She is tall with olive skin that I think is more in keeping with Greece or Spain than Romania. I had expected to see her in a long skirt, a bright colored, billowy peasant blouse, and a bandana around her head. Instead, she is wearing black dress slacks and a red camisole under a black jacket. What strikes me the most about the woman is the serene expression on her face.

"She's even more beautiful than her pictures," Bri gushes.

I give her a brief smile, thinking that she has a crush on the gypsy as I now think of her. For some reason that thought makes me frown. "I hope she will have the answers for you."

"She will. I just know it."

Bri and I are standing toward the back of the room, so I am able to watch as the gypsy approaches each person, giving them a two handed shake and speaking to them.

"Briana, at last we meet," the gypsy says.

It is clear to me that there is a conversation going on between the two of them. Even though I am standing next to Bri, I can't hear a word.

Bri touches my hand and says, "Natasha, this is my friend, Livvy Michelson."

The gypsy grasps my hand between hers, and I can feel a sudden peace come over me. I blink.

"It's a pleasure to meet you," she says in a voice that is so soft I have to strain to hear her. "I've been looking forward to this meeting. We will talk soon."

With that said, she is gone. Her words linger, and I'm sure that what she said is her stock greeting. *What a bunch of crap.* There's no way am I going to let her get her hooks into Briana.

A soft gong rings, and I see everyone heading for the tables. Each place setting has a name card, and Bri and I find that we are sitting at the center of the middle table. I look at my name. "Did you tell someone who you were bringing?"

Bri shook her head. "No."

A waiter wearing white gloves slides a salad in front of me. "Then how did they know my name?"

"Didn't they ask when we came in?" Bri looks at me. "Yes, I'm sure they asked, and I gave them both our names. Dig in, this looks delicious."

I'm not buying that. There wasn't a registration table when we came in, which I remember thinking was odd. No one ever asked us our names or for the tickets. Something fishy is going on, and I don't like it one bit. It is obvious that someone researched Bri and found out who was coming with her. Why would they care? It isn't a stretch to realize how they knew who I was. I have no doubt that this is trickery of some sort to make the people there think that the gypsy is the real deal.

I remember seeing an old black and white movie, *Damnation Alley;* a supposed mind reader gets rich because his partner asks him questions in a way that he knows the answer. *If this charlatan hurts Bri, I will make sure she goes to jail.*

"Don't you think this meal is scrumptious, Livvy?"

I look at Bri who seems so happy. "Yes, it's delicious." I smile. "You got lucky when you got those free tickets."

"I can't wait to speak with her."

I pat her hand. "Just take what she says for what it is—her opinion."

"Oh, I know that. Will you come with me when I speak with her?"

I look at the two chairs that the gypsy and the elderly woman I had seen earlier now occupy. "It looks like it is a one on one, Bri. No room for an extra." I nod toward the gypsy.

Bri appears disappointed. "I was counting on you to be my sounding board." She puts her fork down. "You, I know and trust. Her I trust, but not as much."

"Just take it for what it is, and it will all work out."

Dessert comes just as it is Bri's turn to sit with the gypsy. With great interest, I watch the body language between them. Bri is sitting stiffly in the chair with a grim expression. The gypsy seems relaxed, exuding an air of peace and tranquility. I watch as she leans into Bri and speaks to her. I watch as my friend puts her hand to her mouth. It is obvious she is crying and, for her sake, I hope the gypsy has given her an answer she can live with.

A visibly shaken Bri sits next to me, and I take her hand. "Are you okay?"

"Yes, she said that Sara has been trying to tell me that she loves me and wanted more. She hoped to explore getting married, but when she learned she had cancer, she decided it was best not to tell me. She regrets not telling me and is sorry she had to leave me."

I bite my lip hard to keep from telling Bri that the gypsy is only telling her what she wants to hear. At the same time, it answers the question as to whether Bri will reject my advances. Probably not. *Yes.* Inwardly, I smile.

"Please, come with me," a soft voice says.

I look up to see the man who escorted Bri holding out his hand to me. "Oh, no. I don't need to go up there. I only came to support my friend."

"Please," the man implores.

"Go, Livvy, you'll never know if you don't."

That was an odd thing for Bri to say, but I nod and get up. What can it hurt? I don't believe this crap.

†

I sit in the chair facing the gypsy. Up close, I see just how stunning she is. I'm not going to let a pretty face dissuade me from telling her exactly what I think about this charade. "I don't know what sort of scam you are running here, but don't you mess with my friend in hopes that she will pay you for more of your *insights*."

"It's good to see you again, Livvy. Everyone here has come as my guest. I have never asked for nor accepted money from those I help."

"Bull. Just know that I will be watching you for any sign of underhanded dealings. If I see any and you hurt Bri, I will report you to the authorities."

Natasha smiles. "That is a lovely necklace you are wearing. The design is very intricate."

My hand instinctively encases the necklace. There is no way I'll reveal where it came from.

"There were only two made, and yours is searching for its mate."

"You don't know that," I scoff.

"Your grandmother did."

I stare at the woman in both shock and disbelief. How can she know anything about my grandmother?

"I see you doubt me." She looks out at the others in the room. "You and I need to talk about your grandmother."

"I don't need to talk with you about anything." I start to get up, but she fixes green eyes on me and, for some reason, I am unable to move.

She motions to those sitting at the tables. "Of the twenty people here, you are the one I want to speak with the most."

"You invited Bri, not me, so you had no way of knowing I'd be here."

"Ah, but I did, Livvy. You are why I arranged this gathering."

"That's a load of crap and we both know it."

She tilts her head. "My time is limited right now. I'd like to meet with you in private, so we can discuss your grandmother further. She has a great deal to tell you."

"No way. You guessed that it was from my grandmother. After all, it is old so it couldn't have been a stretch as to where it came from."

"If you'll just meet me again, I will explain everything then."

"I haven't heard anything remotely interesting enough for me to meet you privately." No way am I going to let her know how her comments about my grandmother have rattled me. The more she talks in her calm voice, the more agitated I am becoming. The gypsy reaches out and touches my hand and I want to recoil, but instead I lean into the touch.

"Your grandmother's journal didn't tell the whole story. There is so much more to learn. I can help you find the other one."

Now, she has my attention. "How do you know this?"

144

"Meet with me and you will find out."

I can feel every part of me screaming *yes,* but I fight the feeling. "I'll think about it."

The gypsy hands me a card. "My private number is on the back. Call me, night or day, and I will answer. It is imperative that we talk."

I take the card and stand. "Like I said, I'll think about it."

†

"You two looked chummy up there." Bri looks at me as I retake my seat.

"We did?" It was an odd thing for her to say, since the meeting was so acrimonious.

"Sure, you were laughing while you talked. What was so funny?"

I look at the gypsy who is speaking animatedly with an older woman. I point at them. "Did I look like that?"

"Yes." Bri smiles then frowns. "What's the matter?"

"I just realized that everyone who has sat with her seems to act the same way. I'm wondering if she can make us see only that image."

"You mean like she projects an image that isn't real?"

"Yes. A whole lot of trickery. Magicians today can do amazing things, making us see the unbelievable. Maybe she trained in magic first. Except for you. I could see your reactions. As for me, my time with her was very intense, and funny isn't a word I'd use to describe it, yet you did."

"I told you she's the real deal." Bri is grinning.

I finger the card in my pocket, still reeling from all that the gypsy said. Is she really in contact with my grandmother? How else would she know about the journal? "Yeah, well I'm not so sure, I'd need more proof." I look at the gypsy again and swear I see her smiling at me even though she is talking to someone.

"You should try this baked Alaska."

"What?" I look at the spoon Bri is holding to my lips. I gladly take the offered bite, welcoming her intimate gesture. "Yum, that is really good. What do you say we get out of here and continue this date at my apartment?'

"Best offer I've had all day." She looks at the gypsy who is sitting alone. "Let me tell Natasha good-bye."

I watch as Bri approaches the gypsy and takes her hand. They exchange a few words before they hug.

"Let's go," she says to me upon her return. Bri takes my hand and we begin to leave.

I turn back and see the gypsy looking at me with a somber expression.

†

"Would you like a glass of wine?" I ask after we take off our coats.

"That sounds lovely."

In the kitchen, I pour two glasses of wine before walking back into the living room with them. Bri is sitting in the corner of the couch with her feet tucked under her. Once I give her a glass, I take up the other corner of the couch.

"What did Natasha tell you?" Bri asks.

"Oh, no you don't. This day was about your search for answers. What did she tell you about Sara?"

Bri takes a sip of her wine before putting the glass on the coffee table. She looks at me, opens her mouth, and then closes it. Finally, she says, "As I told you, Sara and I were lifelong friends. When we were in the eleventh grade, we became friends with benefits." I watch as her eyes fix on me before looking away. "That doesn't surprise you?"

"No." I already had the suspicions that she was a lesbian.

"After college, she got a job offer in Boston, and I was all set to go to law school. We kept in touch and, after two years, she moved back here. It wasn't long before we were living together." She takes another sip of her wine and then looks at me. "I thought we were forever."

"Then she got sick?"

"Yes. Everything changed after that. I never took the bar exam." She shrugs. "Sara became distant and eventually moved out of our bedroom. That broke my heart, but I gave her the space she seemed to need. At the time I didn't know how little time we had." She brushes a tear away. "Then she was gone."

"What did...the gyp...Natasha tell you about her?"

Bri smiles. "That although she professed her love for me, she was sorry she shut me out. I already told you that didn't I?"

"Yes." Hearing those words again solidifies my original thoughts about the gypsy. She is a charlatan. Why does that upset me?

"Then she said the most remarkable thing."

My ears perk up. I had no idea there was more. "What was that?"

"That Sara wants me to know that she left something for me in our secret hiding place."

"Does that exist?"

"Oh, yes. In my parent's yard, there's a small building. We once used it as a playhouse. Sara and I had an old cigar box hidden there where we kept things."

"Do you really think anything is there?" I am skeptical about this information.

"Natasha described the cigar box exactly as it was when we put it there. Tomorrow, I am going to go there and see what Sara left for me." She looks at me and leans forward. "Will you go with me?"

"Of course." I'm glad she invites me, since what happens there will tell me whether to call the gypsy or not.

"Thank you. Now, it's your turn."

"For what?"

"Give. What did Natasha say to you?"

I instinctively touch the necklace. "Well, she said my grandmother wants me to know that this pendent," I hold it out, "has a twin, and when I find it I will be complete."

"Wow." She scrunches her forehead. "I've seen something like that before but can't place where."

"Are you sure?"

"Maybe not. It'll probably come to me in the middle of the night." Bri shrugs then smiles. "Were you close to your grandmother?"

"No," I say, shaking my head. "She died before I was born." I feel a chill run up my spine, as I voice the words aloud.

"Was that hers?"

"Yes, my mother gave it to me."

"Did Natasha tell you how to find the twin?"

I shake my head at the incredulity of what I'm going to say. "She told me I was the reason she had the event and that she needs more time to explain everything. I'm supposed to call her and set up an appointment."

"Oh my God, she actually told you that? Did she say why?"

"No. She was very mysterious about it all." I take a sip of my wine. "It probably has to do with the illusion she is trying to create."

"I don't know why you would think that, but I did read that she never gives private readings. You're going to call her aren't you?"

"I don't know. People like that are masters of reading body language. They can ask you a question and know from your reactions as to whether they hit the mark or not. I doubt, seriously, that she can communicate with the dead."

"I guess we will find out tomorrow if she is what she claims to be." Bri looks at her wrist watch. "I better get going. I'll pick you up around nine, if that's okay."

"Will your folks be there?"

"They are in the Caribbean on a cruise and won't be back for another week."

"Do they live close by?"

"It's about an hour's drive to Glen Burnie." Bri grins. "There is a really great diner on the way. I'll buy you breakfast." She stands.

"Sounds good to me." I follow her to the door and pull her into a hug before kissing her cheek. It is a bold move on my part. When she hugs me back, it feels good. Really good. "See you tomorrow."

Chapter Seventeen

The diner we stop at is nothing more than a hole in the wall that I know I'd never consider stopping at, much less eating a meal there. The breakfast is surprisingly good. I'm a pancake junkie and they are light and fluffy.

"Great place, Bri. Do you come here often?"

"Whenever I visit my folks I stop, even if it is only for coffee."

I take a sip of my coffee and savor the flavor. "I can see why. This coffee is some of the best I've ever tasted."

Bri laughs. "My mom always wants me to bring her a cup." She looks at her watch. "I guess I've stalled long enough."

"You're nervous, aren't you?" I reach across the table and take her hand. "I'll be right there with you, no matter what."

"I'm counting on that." She turns her hand over and laces our fingers. "Thank you."

I feel my cheeks heat up. "Come on, let's get going."

We get to our feet and head for the door. I'm worried for Bri, since I don't have much faith in the gypsy or her predictions. I'm not sure how she knew about my grandmother, but I will figure out her trick eventually.

✝

Bri's family lives in a two-story colonial home nestled at the top of a hill on an acre lot surrounded by tulip poplars and white pines. She drives her car up the driveway and parks in front of a three-car garage.

"Have you always lived here?" I ask after we get out of the car.

"We moved here when I was two, so the answer is no, but it's the only home I've ever known."

"It looks like a great place to grow up."

"Yes, it was. What was your growing up home like?"

"It's your typical California home. It isn't as big as this one, and the lot is much smaller." I look at Bri and smile. "You're stalling again."

"I know," she whispers.

Ever since we left the diner, Bri hasn't said much, and I can tell she is anxious about what she'll find. "Where's the playhouse?"

"Out back by the pool. Once we all left home, my mom made it into a pool house."

"Oh. Do you think your secret hiding place is still there?"

"Yes. If anyone found it, they'd have let me know. In my family there are no secrets. I'm surprised we were able to keep the cigar box under wraps all this time." She takes my hand. "Come on. Let's go find out if Natasha is the real deal or not."

"Don't get your hopes up." I finger the gypsy's card in my pocket. If this is a wild goose chase, I am going to call

151

her and make sure she knows just how much she's hurt my friend.

"Don't worry, Livvy, I know the chances of finding anything are slim." We stop in front of a small building, and Bri takes out a key, unlocks the door, and steps inside. "I'm always amazed at how much smaller this seems. Growing up, it was enormous."

I watch as Bri walks to the back of the building, bends down, and lifts a floor board. She pulls out an old cigar box that looks like it has seen better days. "Is that it?"

"Yes. Come over here and be with me when I open it."

Once there, I can see her hands trembling. "Do you want me to look first?"

Bri shakes her head. "No. Just stay by my side."

"I will."

She lifts the lid and, inside, I see a pack of cigarettes, a bundle of notes wrapped in a ribbon, a small bottle of tequila, and a black velvet bag."

"This wasn't in here the last time I looked." She takes the bag out and, with her shaking fingers, opens it. Inside are what look like a ring box and note. She unfolds the note and closes her eyes briefly. "It's from Sara."

I wait, watching various emotions flicker across her face.

She clears her throat and begins reading.

"My, darling, if you are reading this then I am gone and you are alone. I'm sorry that I had to leave you, but please know that I am always with you, watching over you. Before I became ill, I bought this for you. Please wear it as a remembrance of my love for you. Always Yours, Sara."

Bri folds the note and opens the ring box. Inside is a Claddagh wedding ring. "Before she got sick, we were planning on going to Ireland," she whispers with tears slowly rolling down her cheeks. "Why did she leave me?"

I didn't know what to say. My heart is breaking for her, and I take her in my arms, holding her close. "Go ahead and cry. I've got you and won't let go." After a few moments, Bri pulls back and looks at me. Her kisses are hungry and insistent and, lost in the moment, I return them.

"Love me," she pleads.

I can sense her pain and, although I know it is wrong, I give her what she needs willingly. "Not here." The floor of a shack isn't where I'd imagined Bri and I making love for the first time.

✝

Bri takes my hand and leads me to the house where she unlocks the back door and we walk inside. Together, we go up the staircase and down a hallway to a bedroom.

"This is my room." She pulls me to her and kisses me again.

I pull back and hold her face in my hands. "Bri, are you sure?"

"Yes. It will be a fantasy come true." Her hands find their way under my t-shirt, and then she lifts it over my head.

Standing naked in front of Bri, I shiver not from a chill but from the anticipation of what is to come. Again, I ask, "Are you sure?"

Bri pushes me back onto the bed and straddles my hips before bending and kissing me passionately. As she stretches the length of her body over me, I feel her skin against mine for the first time. It has been far too long since feeling a naked woman's body touching mine, and I savor the moment.

My fingers caress her back, eliciting a soft moan which encourages me to explore further. My lips find hers, and I run my tongue along them. She responds by opening her mouth. The kisses deepen, and I roll her over so I can gaze at her luscious body with all the right curves right where they are the most delectable.

"You are so beautiful," I whisper before taking a swollen nipple between my lips and squeezing it tenderly. Her hand grips my head and holds it in place. She squeals, as my fingers find their way down her body. I splay my fingers over her mound before slipping them slowly through her hot, wet center.

Bri raises her hips with each stroke of my fingers through the velvety wetness, and I suck on her nipple harder.

"Please," she begs.

I lift my head and look at her, seeing the want and the need on her face. Slowly, I begin kissing my way down her body. I can smell her need and want to taste it. My lips surround the hard nub, and I take it in my mouth as three fingers slide inside her.

Bri is bucking so hard that I must grab her with my free hand to keep licking and sucking. I curl my fingers inside her, while drawing her clit in farther. She screams and lifts her hips, holding them in place as her body trembles with release.

I remain between her legs, running my tongue slowly along the length of her, as small tremors continue until she finally sighs.

"Come up here," she says.

I comply, and it isn't long before our kisses heat up once again and Bri begins her exploration of my body.

It is late afternoon when we finally get out of bed. "Are you okay?" I ask.

"Yes. Thank you for being here for me."

I pull her close and encircle her waist with my arms. "Does this make us friends with benefits?"

"Would you like that?"

"Yes, I think I would. You have to admit that what we just shared was amazing."

Bri looks away. "Yes, it was and that scares me."

I kiss her neck. "Why?"

"After Sara died, I made a vow not to let my heart get so involved that it would break again." She shrugs. "I can't offer you more than friends with benefits. I'm sorry."

"Hey, don't be sorry. That's what I want too."

"Are you sure?"

I walk her back to the bed and we fall on it together. "Yes, I'm sure. Let me show you how much."

†

On the ride to my apartment, we hold hands and when I glance at her she has what I'd say is a look of happiness.

"So, what did you think of Natasha?" Bri asks.

"Not sure. She was right about Sara, and it freaks me out that she knew about my grandmother."

"So you think she is really who she says she is?"

I consider her question and bite my lip. "Not sure. I think there is some form of trickery involved."

"Oh, Livvy, how can you say that? The box was exactly where she said it would be. How else would she know about it?"

"I'm not sure, but I *will* figure it out." I squeeze her hand. "Will you spend the night?"

Bri shakes her head. "I wish I could, but Sundays are my laundry day and I've got a mountain to do or I'll be wearing day-old underwear tomorrow."

"I can fix that. I have an unopened package you can use."

"Tempting as that sounds, I really do like my routine, and if I don't do the laundry my whole week will be off."

"Fair enough." I lean in and kiss her cheek. "I can get a kiss good night, can't I?"

"Count on it."

Chapter Eighteen

Hearing a knock on my office door, I look up and see Bri standing in the doorway. A smile fills her beautiful freckled face, and her red hair that she usually wears in a ponytail is down and kissing her shoulders. I shiver as I remember making love to her on Saturday.

"Busy?"

"No. Come on in, please."

Bri walks into my office, closes the door, and comes to stand beside me, resting against my desk. "I wanted to make sure you were okay."

I run a finger down her thigh. "I'm fabulous. What about you? Regrets?"

"None at all. I want to see you again. Take you out on a proper date."

"I think that can be arranged." I wrap my arm around her waist and pull her close. "Is it okay if I kiss you?"

"I'd like that, but I didn't lock the door."

I smile and shrug. "I'll chance it if you will." Bri bends down, and I hungrily meet her lips as the kiss intensifies. My phone rings and we break apart. *Damn.* "Hello," I say more gruffly than I mean to. "Yes, pencil me in for two o'clock. Okay, thank you."

Bri moves around to the other side of my desk. "I think we need some distance, or we will have to lock the door." She smirks and then sighs.

"It's less than fifteen minutes to my apartment. We could take an early lunch."

"Tempting as that sounds, I have a meeting in ten minutes and then I have to catch Phil Baker up on the latest results."

"Then will you go to dinner with me tonight?" I didn't want to sound desperate, but I couldn't help myself.

"I'd love to." She smiles, then her face gets serious. "Did you call Natasha yet?"

I look at her hand—she is wearing Sara's ring. We are only friends with benefits, so why does seeing that upset me so? "No. It completely slipped my mind."

"I think you should call her. After all, the fact that we found the ring proves that she is not a fake." She lifts her hand and looks at the ring.

"You're right." I pull the card out of my bag along with my cell phone, dial the number, and put it on speaker. "Hello, Natasha? This is…"

"Livvy. I was wondering when you'd call."

"Sorry, life got a bit complicated." I look at Bri and lift an eyebrow before grinning.

"Ah, so you found the ring, Briana."

I look at Bri and frown. "Yes, I did," she says.

"Sara is very happy. Did you read the inscription?"

"Yes." Bri stands there with a blank look on her face before wiping away a tear.

I walk around the desk, hug her close, and kiss her cheek lightly. "You said we should speak in private and I wanted to set up a time," I tell Natasha.

"Unfortunately, Livvy, I'm leaving this evening for Paris and will be gone for at least a month."

"Oh, I left it too long then." A part of me is relieved another disappointed.

"No, you didn't. This is a last minute trip that I am obliged to make. I will meet with you when I get back."

"Okay. Just call me when you are ready." I don't think I disguised my indifference at the turn of events. Yet something inside of me is screaming that I'm wrong about her. I push the thought aside.

"Livvy?"

"Yes."

"Your grandmother wants you to know that great joy awaits you."

I look at Bri and wink. "Yes, I know that."

"I must go now. Just remember that all is not always as it seems. I will call you when I am back. Bye for now."

The gypsy hangs up before I can reply. "Wonder what she meant by that. Hell, maybe she was talking about herself."

"I wonder how she knew I was here and you had the speaker on."

"Enough about her." The last thing I want to discuss is the gypsy. "Where do you want to have dinner tonight? Your choice."

Bri grins. "I want you to cook for me."

"Good answer." I pull her closer and kiss her lips. "I'll amaze you with my culinary skills."

"Along with your other skills." She runs a finger down my arm and wiggles her eyebrows.

"Most definitely."

†

Over the next four weeks Bri and I see each other outside of the office often. I have meetings in DC for a week but manage to get back and be with her two of the five nights I am gone. The more I am with her, the more feelings other than friendship begin developing. I find myself eager to go to work every morning, knowing that I'll see Bri and that we'll make time to be together. When my phone rings, I pick it up, smiling, expecting to hear Bri's voice.

"Livvy, this is Natasha Gabor."

"Oh, hi." Disappointment laces my words.

"I arrived back in the States early this morning, and I wanted to touch base with you about setting up a meeting."

I don't need this gypsy derailing my life. I have something positive going on with Bri, and I really don't want to hear some mumbo jumbo about my grandmother and some true love waiting for me. "Look, I appreciate your contacting me, but I'm not in a position to meet with you."

"Your grandmother—"

"My grandmother is dead. I said I'm not interested. You may or may not be in contact spiritually with my grandmother, I don't know and don't care. My life is going along just fine, and I don't need your input. Thank you and good-bye." I am just about to hang up when I hear her speak.

"Will you please just hear me out?" Her voice softens, taking on a pleading tone.

"Why should I?"

"Because, if I don't see this to the end I will never know any peace."

"That's not my problem, Ms. Gabor."

"You, your grandmother, the other woman, and I are all connected."

I'm momentarily taken aback and shiver at the sound of the reference to who could only be Jac. *How does she know this?* "I don't believe you."

160

"Meet with me, and I will show you positive proof."

I look up, see Bri standing in the doorway, and wave her in with a smile. "What kind of game are you playing?"

"Matters of the heart are never a game to me."

Her voice is so soft that I almost don't hear what she says. It's then that something clicks, telling me I have no choice, and I know in that moment that I will meet her. "Tell me when and where."

"Tomorrow evening at the Kimpton Hotel Monaco in DC. Do you know where it is?"

"I can find it."

"Will seven give you enough time to get here? The majority of the traffic should be leaving the city so the drive in shouldn't be difficult."

"It will be Friday night and I suspect the traffic will be bad, but I will be there at seven."

"Thank you. I'll see you then."

"Good-bye." I hang up and look at Bri. "You'll never guess who that was."

"An old girlfriend that has come to town and wants to see you?"

"No. It was Natasha."

"She's back in town?"

"Yes, and she's very insistent that I meet with her. You want to come along?"

Bri, standing at my desk, lets out a sigh. "No. I think this is something you need to do on your own. You can solve the mystery of your grandmother." She leans across the desk. "I know it has been eating at you."

I was there for her when she found Sara's ring, but she is refusing to support me in this. Unbelievable. "No it hasn't." I fight to keep the disappointment from my voice.

Bri raises an eyebrow.

"Okay, maybe a little bit." I nervously shuffle some papers on my desk. "Want to spend the weekend with me? We can go to the coast and spend some alone time there." I wiggle my eyebrows.

"I can't. I promised Elaine Brooks that I'd help her get moved in."

"Elaine Brooks?" I know I've heard the name before. "Oh, the new hire. I didn't know you two were friendly."

"I got to know her last week while you were in DC."

A vision of the petite blonde came to mind. Cute is the only word I can think to describe her. "I see."

Bri walks over and closes the door before coming back to stand next to me. "She's nice and there's something there. I can't quite explain how she makes me feel, but it is something that I want to explore." Her eyes seem to be imploring me to understand. "I need to do this, Livvy."

"I understand." I look at her face and see mixed emotions playing there. I have to look away. This is a rejection I didn't see coming. Not so soon anyway. The depth of it hurts more than anything I've experienced before.

"You hate me don't you?"

"No. We agreed to be friends with benefits until the right one came along. I get it. Your face lit up just now when you said her name. I'm happy for you." I'm reeling from her rejection, and I try hard not to let it show.

"I'm sorry. I never meant to hurt you," she says.

"I'm sure you didn't." I can't keep my voice from sounding cold.

"Livvy—"

"No, don't make this any more difficult than it is, Bri. I know we agreed to be friends with benefits, but I really thought we were growing closer." I let out a sigh. "Obviously, that was one-sided."

She bends down and kisses my cheek. "I'm so sorry."

Her voice is working on my last nerve and I want to scream *get out of here,* but before I can my phone rings. "I have to get this." *Saved by the bell.*

Bri shrugs, mouths *I'm sorry,* and leaves.

"Hello." I begin listening to a recording drone on about how I can save on my credit cards before I end the call. Leaning back in my chair, I shake my head. "Damn. I didn't see that one coming." I had really thought that we were going beyond the friend's stage into something more meaningful. "Fuck. Where is chocolate-chocolate chunk ice cream when I need it?"

Chapter Nineteen

The Kimpton Hotel Monaco is opulent, to say the least. I look around the esthetically pleasing lobby for the gypsy. Suddenly, she is by my side, seemingly coming out of nowhere.

"I am so glad that you came." She takes my arm with a gentle touch. "Come, we will go to my suite. Dinner will be arriving soon."

"I didn't know we'd be having dinner."

"Nothing fancy. It's just something light."

†

The gypsy's suite is like nothing I've ever seen before. Where the lobby is opulent, the room is luxurious. "Wow!"

"I'm glad you like it." Natasha looks at me before smiling. "I'm not a gypsy."

"Your name suggests otherwise." I see a twinkle in her eyes.

"It is a stage name to add an air of mystery around

164

me."

"What is your real name then?"

She waggles a finger at me. "Tonight is about you."

There is a soft knock at the door and she opens it to a man dressed in black pants, a white shirt, and a vest. He rolls a table into the room and sets covered plates on a table with a white cloth before uncovering them.

"Is this satisfactory?" he asks the gypsy.

"Yes, George, it is perfect as always."

The man leaves, and the gypsy motions toward the table. "Please, join me."

I reluctantly move to the table, and when I see the cob salad, my stomach rumbles. "This looks delicious."

"As I said, it's something light."

While I eat, I look cautiously at the gypsy who is looking at me intently. I wonder what she has up her sleeve to try to persuade me that what she is telling me is the truth. "If you want me to believe you are not a charlatan, then you will have to convince me."

"Fair enough. I will answer one question as long as it isn't what my real name is."

What is it about her name that she doesn't want to reveal it to me? I guess I'll have to make my one question count then. "Okay, when did you first know you could communicate with the dead?"

"When I was fifteen, I was struck by lightning. My heart stopped and I died. My aunt, who was there with my mother, had just completed a first aid course for CPR and she brought me back to life. She told me later that all the time she was doing the chest compressions she could feel the energy of the lightning in my body seeping into her. Later, in the hospital, when I regained consciousness, I opened my eyes and it was as if a cacophony of voices was bombarding my mind." She looks at me. "Have you ever been in a room full of people and they are all talking loudly at once and you hear the drone of their voices but never their words?"

"Yes." I am finding her story unbelievable, yet strangely compelling.

"That was what my life was like for the next few months. There was a constant humming of voices in my head." She rubs her temple. "I thought I was going mad. When I finally told my mother what was happening, she took me to a psychiatrist who gave me drugs—they didn't help. It became so bad that my mother had to home school me, because I couldn't function in a school setting." She lifts a shoulder. "The more people that were around me the worse it was."

"Then what happened?"

"A year later, she took me to a psychic and my world changed."

"In what way?" I ask skeptically. Now we are getting somewhere. Finally, the gypsy's mumbo jumbo that I suspect is behind all of this is unfolding.

"She helped me to listen to the voices, sort through them, and quieten them." Her eyes then focus on me. "That's why I was able to hear your grandmother's voice."

"Really? And when was that?" I have to smile. This is ludicrous on so many levels that I can't believe I'm still sitting here.

The gypsy stares over my shoulder, and I can't stop myself from looking around to see if someone is there. There isn't. I wait to hear what her next line of bullshit is.

"About five years ago, I was in Dallas for a book signing. I was on my way to the airport, traveling down Interstate 820. Traffic was backed up for miles, and as my car crept along the road, I was suddenly overcome with a voice pleading for me to listen.

The gypsy looks at me with a distressed look on her

face. "It was your grandmother. She wanted me to find you and give you a message."

I want to laugh, but the seriousness on her face makes me stop. "And what is that?"

"That love is there waiting for you to return."

"Return? You must have me mixed up with someone else. I've never been in love, so there is nothing to return to." For a moment, I wonder if she is referring to Bri. Maybe not all is lost where she is concerned.

"It's there waiting for you," she continues. "All you need to do is open your heart to the possibility, Livvy. When you find the other locket, you'll know the truth."

"And I suppose you know where that is."

The gypsy nods, then a smile that I can only describe as serene fills her face. "She wants you to meet Jac."

Although she had mentioned the name before, the comment surprises me. "That will be hard to do since all I have is a first name. I've looked for her and have come up empty at every turn."

"She's waiting for you."

"This is way too cryptic for me." I stand to go. "I've got more important things to do than listen to this load of crap. Thanks for the food it was delicious, so this evening wasn't all a waste."

"I'll be waiting to hear from you again, Livvy. Don't leave it too long, for Jac's days are few."

"Whatever." I practically run to the door and after opening it, I speed walk to the elevator. "Crazy gypsy."

†

The door to my apartment closes behind me and I lock it, hoping to stop the replay of my conversation with the gypsy. I need to talk to someone so I can straighten out all

167

the confusing thoughts I'm having. The only real friend I have here is Bri, and I thought the gypsy referred to not giving up on her. I can't believe that I'm pulling my phone out of my back pocket. Bri has made it clear how she feels, yet on the advice of the gypsy who I am dubious about, I am dialing her number. After six rings, I realize that she isn't there and start to hang up.

"Hello."

I've heard that breathless sound from Bri many times before and know she isn't alone. "Sorry, I didn't mean to interrupt," I say quickly. "I'll see you on Monday. Bye." Not giving her a chance to speak, I press end and hold the phone limply in my hand. My cheeks grow hot with embarrassment. "I used to make her sound like that. Damn, who do I talk to now?"

I think about calling my mom. I know that she is still sensitive when it comes to talking about her mother, and I don't want to burden her more. The last thing she needs is to hear about some crackpot gypsy. In retrospect, I realize that because I had Bri I hadn't bothered to cultivate any newer friends—now, I regret my choices.

Going into the kitchen, I take a wine glass out of the cupboard and then open the refrigerator door. I spy an open bottle of Toasted Head Chardonnay, grab it, and uncork the bottle, before taking it and the glass into the living room.

Snippets of the conversation with the gypsy invade my thoughts so randomly they annoy me, and I try to ignore them but they remain insistent. How did she know that my grandmother died in Dallas on the exact highway she mentioned? Surely, a deadly car crash that happened more than twenty years ago wouldn't be on the internet. *Or would it?* Impossible, crashes like that happen all the time. I wrack my brain trying to remember if she ever said my grandmother's last name. I can't remember. I look around for my laptop it's in my bedroom and I decide against checking—for now.

The words—it's there waiting for you, all you need to do is open your heart to the possibility—keep pushing their way to the top of my consciousness. Then on the fringes of my memory, something the gypsy said as I was leaving is trying to have a voice. "What is it that she said?"

After gulping down the rest of the wine in my glass, I pour more hoping it will chase away all the thoughts jumbling up my mind. All I get is a fuzzy, tired brain. I look at the clock and see that it is almost midnight. "Time for bed. I'll figure this all out in the morning."

Once I snuggle under the sheets, my eyes grow heavy, and I thankfully let sleep over take my troubled mind. I bolt straight up in bed. The sheets tangled around me make me struggle to free myself. The words I've been trying to remember are clear. *Don't leave it too long, for Jac's days are few.*

"Jac's alive!"

Chapter Twenty

I pace the kitchen holding my phone to my ear. "Come on, answer." The gypsy has been so eager for me to talk with her, so why isn't she answering the phone now?

"Hello, Livvy."

"Is it true? Is Jac alive?"

"Good morning to you too. I knew you would call, and I'm sorry you were awake all night. You could have called me then."

"Listen, you led me down this road, so I'd appreciate an answer." I hear the sound of my voice and close my eyes at the harshness of it. "I'm sorry," I whisper. "I've been awake most of the night, waiting to call you about Jac."

"I knew you would call. Yes, Jac is alive."

"When can I see her?"

"She's frail, and I will not allow you to upset her."

"I mean her no harm, Natasha. All I want to do is find out more about my grandmother." My voice sounds as weary as I feel. "Please, let me see her."

"Very well. I will text you the address and meet you there at noon."

After I end the call, I suddenly get a sick feeling of apprehension about what I might find. It fills my mind, and my body begins to shake.

✝

I take a deep breath, as I get out of my car that I parked in the lot of the Sunset Senior Living Center. In the distance, I look at the entrance to the building and don't see the gypsy. I wonder, not for the first time, if she is playing me. Nevertheless, I make my way to the door. Since I don't know Jac's last name, I'll ask for a resident named Jacqueline who is, I think, in her seventies. How many women can that be in what looks like a small, well-kept facility?

The gypsy is waiting inside the building for me and that surprises me.

"I didn't think you were here."

"I've been here for a while. I needed to make sure she was able to have company. She had chemo yesterday, and the next day is always tough on her."

The comment surprises me. "I didn't know."

"How would you? It's not working and it looks like hospice will start sooner rather than later."

For some reason, I feel my heart shudder at her words. "May I see her?"

"Yes. I told her she has a visitor."

The room is dark, but I can make out a figure lying in a bed. A light goes on, and I can see that, despite her age and infirmity, the woman is clearly beautiful. She looks at me, and her eyes widen before closing. I instinctively know this is Jac.

"Carol, you came back to me." Jac reaches out to me.

"I'm Livvy, Carol's granddaughter."

171

She gives me a confused look. "But isn't your name Carol?"

"Yes, but everyone calls me Livvy." I can't take my eyes off her, for she looks so familiar to me. "Have we met before?"

"Gray, please give us a moment alone."

I look at the gypsy. "Gray?"

"Natasha is my stage name, my real name is Grayson."

"And you know Jac how?" I ask.

"She's my aunt."

"The one that saved your life?" I watch as the gypsy nods. All the pieces fall into place and I just stare at the woman. "That's how you knew all about my grandmother." I can feel my body beginning to react in anger and I temper it. "Did you get all the information about me so you could dupe me into thinking the impossible?" I know I am acting like a child, but everything is too coincidental to not reach this conclusion. I begin moving away.

"Stop! You promised not to upset her." Gray tells me in a hushed tone.

"No! I told her nothing." Jac's previously frail sounding voice booms out and I turn to her. "Please, hear me out."

I can hear the desperation in her voice and see the sincerity in her eyes. She loved my grandmother enough to let her go, and I doubt she would do anything underhanded to hurt her granddaughter. I feel all the air go out of my body and am ashamed that my words upset her. "Please, tell me."

"When Gray first honed her skills at talking to the dead, I told her if she ever ran across someone named Carol Barngate to tell her I love her. That is all I ever said to her."

"Why should I believe either of you?" Anger is consuming me. How could I have been so stupid?

"Because Carol is the love of my life, and I would never do anything to harm her or you. Gray told me, five years ago, that she'd made contact with your grandmother who told her to find you." Her blue eyes seem to be beseeching me to understand.

"I'm sorry, I find this all so surreal, but I will listen to you with an open mind."

Again, she holds out her hand to me. "Please, come and sit with me. I've so much to tell you, and my time is nearing its end."

Her voice is soft, and I can hear something else in it—desperation. With hesitant steps, I move toward the bed, and she takes my hand. Considering the gravity of her health, the warmth of her hand surprises me.

"Please, sit."

I comply and watch as she nods at her niece who leaves the room.

"Gray only has good intentions where you are concerned."

"I find that hard to believe. It seems to me that she has been trying to manipulate me ever since I first met her."

"The name Grayson means someone who is rare with the ability to love with all their heart. She means you no harm and, contrary to what you think, she isn't a gypsy."

"Okay. What is it that you want to tell me?" To my ears, I sound gruff and I instantly regret my tone. "Please, tell me about her," I say in a softer voice.

"From the moment I saw her, I knew she was the one who would fill the void in my heart."

"Sexually?"

"No. It wasn't like that. Not that I didn't want that. I did. But trying to lure her away from her family just wasn't right."

"Very noble of you."

"Not noble. It was the right thing to do." Her eyes fix on me. "There is only one choice when you do what's right and millions of choices for doing the wrong thing."

"I know. I've read the letters you sent her and her journal. Please, tell me what it was like for you."

"All consuming is the best description. Your grandmother made me want to be a better person. Before I met Carol, I wasn't a very nice person," she shrugs, "a player who put my needs above all else. After meeting her, I began seeing everything from a kinder, gentler place. When I lost her, I became hollow in here." She touches her heart and sighs. "I've learned to live without her, but she is always with me. She became the endless dream that I keep reaching for but is always just a fingertip away."

"If that's what love does to a person, I'm not sure I want any part of it."

"It is worth everything to love." Her fingers caress my cheek. "You look so much like her that it is almost like she is sitting here with me. Of course, lately I've seen her standing by the door waiting for me. Gray was here one day and through her I was able to speak with your grandmother."

"I'm sorry. I find it difficult to believe in the afterlife."

"She's worried about you." Jac's voice still sounds strong.

"Who? Your niece?"

"No, your grandmother."

"That's impossible. She doesn't even know me."

"You're wrong. She was there when you were born and touched you with her soul."

I can see Jac's eyes seemingly searching me and I nod, knowing in my heart that her words are true. "All my life I've thought I had a guardian angel watching over me," I whisper.

Her fingers touch my grandmother's necklace. "I remember when I had that made for her. I wanted her to always be reminded of my love, just as the one I had reminded me of hers." She smiles. "Now you have it and once you find the other half, you will know the love we shared."

"And how will I find it? I haven't a clue as to where to start looking." Inwardly I am shaking my head that I'm even having this conversation, but something tells me that her words are true.

"Aristotle said, 'Love is composed of a single soul inhabiting two bodies.' All you have to do, my sweet girl, is be open to the possibility."

"What does that mean? It sounds like an unsolvable riddle to me. Can't you just tell me?" My voice is sharper than I want. "Please," I say softly.

Jac closes her eyes and becomes very still. I wonder if she's fallen asleep. The gypsy enters the room at that moment.

"That's all she can do for today," she whispers.

"But—"

"She's given you all she can for now. Please, understand how frail she is."

The sincerity of her words makes me acquiesce, and I look at Jac then at her niece. "How did you know to come in now?"

"When she brought me back to life, our souls melded and we've been in sync ever since."

"Huh," I say following her out of the room. My stomach rumbles so loud that I think I hear it echo off the walls.

"Are you hungry?" she asks with a smirk.

"Yeah, I guess I am. I was so nervous about today that I haven't eaten since yesterday at lunch."

"Come on then. I know a great burger joint about a block away. We can walk and won't have to worry about finding a place to park."

"I've taken up too much of your time already. I'll just head on back home and get something along the way."

"Nonsense. My treat."

"Well, I do have questions that maybe you can answer, and I would like to know more."

"Come on then." She holds out her hand and I take it, shivering at the touch.

†

When I walk into The Terrier restaurant, it is like going back in time. Pictures of movie stars from the early years of film mix with antiques to adorn the walls. I've seen other restaurants decorated in a similar fashion, but something about the place washes over my body with pleasure.

"Wow." I smile at the gypsy. "This place is amazing."

"Wait until you taste the burgers. They grind their own grass fed and finished beef and cook them to order. So you can have the medium rare hamburger you like."

How does she know that?

"Come on, I see an empty table over there." She points to the far corner of the area.

After sitting down, I look at the woman across from me. "I've never been here before, but somehow it feels familiar. How did you know I like medium rare?"

She merely smiles at my question.

"My Aunt Jac turned me on to this place. She told me that she and her special friend, Carol, came here when your grandmother was in DC for a conference."

"Please, tell me the truth. Did you know everything about my grandmother because your aunt told you?" I look directly into her eyes, knowing I'll see her deceit if it's there, because I can feel a bond developing between us.

"Your grandmother channeled through me to speak with Aunt Jac. What they said to each other had nothing to do with you."

"Pardon me if I tell you I don't believe you."

She shrugs. "That's your prerogative. I can't..." Gray closes her eyes and nods before opening them and staring at me. "She's gone," she whispers.

A sense of apprehension fills me, and I know the answer. Nevertheless, I frown and ask, "Who? Not Jac."

"Yes, Jac."

"How do you know that?"

"She just came to me and said that they were together again."

Her phone rings, and I listen to the one-sided conversation. "Hello... Yes, I understand..." She furrows her forehead. "You should have all her directives... Yes, please call her and let her know..." Gray nods before rubbing her eyes. "Thank you, good-bye." She looks at me. "That was her nurse. She went in to check on her after we left, and she was gone." Gray blew out a breath. "She said my aunt had a smile on her face."

Instinctively, I reach across the table and cover her hand with mine. "I'm so sorry. Is there anything I can do for you?"

"No. I need to go back and say good-bye to her."

Tears are stinging my eyes. "May I come with you?" I don't understand what has come over me. I did not know Jac other than what I read in the journal and in her letters, yet I feel as though my heart is ripping into a million parts. I look across the table and see that Gray is just sitting there. I push my chair back and go to her.

"Come on, you shouldn't go alone."

"Thank you," she says softly. "I'll be all right."

"I want to say good-bye too." The truth behind my words startles me. "If you'll let me."

Her chair scrapes along the floor. "Come on then, we don't have much time."

†

Gray kisses her aunt's cheek and smiles. "She's still warm." Gray turns to me. "They are both here."

I look around the room and think for one moment I can feel them then dismiss it. I must be channeling the moment. It is the first time I've seen someone who has just passed away.

"Their joy is palpable. Can you feel it, Livvy?"

I don't want to lie, but she looks so hopeful, I debate what answer I will give her. "For a moment, I thought I did but then it was gone."

Gray comes over to me and touches my hand. "Relax and let the energy flow through you. They so want to touch you with their love."

My initial reaction is fear, but when I see the hope in her eyes, I close mine and concentrate on her hand. Suddenly, a warm sensation begins in my fingers and is soon coursing through my entire body. Love is engulfing me, body and soul. It is so overwhelming that I can feel its warmth. I open my eyes and see Gray smiling at me.

"You felt it didn't you?"

"Yes. It was a combination of peace and love." The heat of the moment lingers, and I want to cry out with joy.

"They want you to know that once you find your other half you will feel the love they shared too."

The emotions of the moment get to me and I begin sobbing. "I don't know where to look."

"Be open to the possibilities, Livvy."

Just then, the door swings open and a woman who resembles Jac, somewhat, walks quickly to the bed. She holds her hand over her mouth and cries softly. "Were you with her, Gray?"

"Shortly before. She chose to go quietly and alone."

"I wish I'd been here. At least now she no longer is suffering."

"She wants you to know that she loves you, Mom, and that she will always be with you. She is happy now."

"Is she with Carol?"

"Yes."

At that moment, the woman notices me and frowns. "Who are you and what are you doing here?" She wipes away her tears. "This is a private moment and we don't need you here. Please, leave."

I get that this woman doesn't want me in her sister's room. She has every right to ask me to leave, for I am an intruder in what is a private family moment. "I'm sorry," I say and go to the door.

"Livvy, wait, don't go," Gray says.

I walk out the door and quickly go to the exit. The last twenty-four hours have been the day from hell, and I brush away tears. I press the button to open my car and get in. I am a confused, emotional mess. As I drive out of the parking lot, I see Gray standing at the entrance, watching me.

I keep going.

On my way home, I engage the hands free button and call my mom.

"Hi. I was just thinking about you," Mom says when she answers. I can hear the smile in her voice.

"Mom, I found Jac," I blurt out.

"Oh."

"She died a few hours ago." I can't keep the sorrow from my voice.

"Did you get to speak to her?"

"Yes."

"Hey, what's going on?" Mom's voice is soft and compassionate. "Tell me all about it."

Glad to have someone to talk to, I begin to tell her about going with Bri to the gypsy event and everything after that.

"Sounds like you've had a rough time of it. Do you need me to visit?"

"As tempting as that sounds, I think I'll hold off calling that one in. Now that Jac is gone, I don't expect I'll have any more contact with Gray."

"Ah, I wondered if she had a name. She's no longer the gypsy?"

I laugh for the first time in quite a while. "No. I know, now, she isn't a gypsy, and I am convinced she is who she says she is and can do what she says she can do."

"That's good to hear. Does Bri think the same?"

"I really don't know." I gulp back a sob. "She's found someone else."

"Oh, darling, are you sure you don't want me to visit?"

"Not right now, but thanks for asking." I pull my car into a free slot in front of my apartment. "I'm home now and the tub is calling my name."

"Okay. Have a good night."

"I will. Thanks, Mom, bye."

"Livvy?"

"Yes."

"I'm glad you called and told me about Jac."

"Me too. I guess we've put that mystery to rest."

"Yes, we have."

"Bye, Mom, I love you."

Chapter Twenty-one

On Monday morning, Bri comes into my office and closes the door. "Why did you hang up on me?"

"You were obviously busy, and I was sorry I interrupted you and what's-her-name." I say petulantly.

"As it turns out, she isn't all I expected her to be."

"Yeah right, you sounded like you were having a really horrible time. I've heard you sound like that, Bri." I start sorting through a folder on my desk. "If that's all, I've got work to do."

Bri pulls up a chair next to me. "Please tell me why you called. You saw Natasha, didn't you?"

"I did." I can feel the heat of her body, and the familiar longing I have when she's around makes an appearance.

"Tell me." She reaches over and caresses my cheek. "Please."

"Don't." I push her hand away. "I was upset Friday night and needed to talk to someone. I realize that you can't be that person ever again."

"You can always talk to me, Livvy, we are friends." She takes my chin and turns my head so I am facing her.

"Nothing will change that, ever."

"You know, you could have told me and not blind-sided me like that. One day we are lovers, the next I find I've been replaced." I narrow my eyes. "That hurt, Bri."

"I'm sorry. I wasn't sure that you would appreciate me having more than one friend with benefits. It's a bit like a ménage à trois. I want to keep your friendship, so I figured it was better to tell you as soon as it happened."

"You are right, I wouldn't. Fine. I'm happy for you. Now, if you don't mind, I have a pile of scenarios to work on."

"I'm not leaving until you tell me about what upset you. I still believe we are good friends to share stuff. Tell me I'm wrong."

I rub a hand over my face and eventually nod. "So much happened that there isn't enough time right now to talk about it. All I can say is that I was upset on Friday night but by Saturday, I was more confused than anything else. Since I couldn't talk to you, I called my mom and we had a good chat."

"I'm sorry I wasn't there for you."

"I dealt with it."

"Next time give me the benefit of the doubt."

I look directly at her. "I can't do this now, Bri. Maybe another day." I see a dejected look before she leaves my office. As I watch the door close, I know that any notion I had that Bri is the one no longer exists.

Remembering Jac's words about being open to the possibility, I open my phone and text Gray. *Is it okay if I come to Jac's funeral?* Several hours pass without a response, and I take that to mean she'd rather I don't attend. Under the circumstances that is understandable.

†

182

It is almost ten o'clock. I'm getting ready for bed and my phone rings. "What now?" Phones that ring late at night or during the night are usually a bad thing. It's almost seven in California, so if it's Mom or Dad maybe it isn't bad news.

I pick up my cell and don't recognize the number. "Damn telemarketers." I'm about to chuck the phone onto my bed but change my mind. I've had a really rotten last few days and I need to vent.

"Hello! Do you have any idea how late it is?"

"Livvy, this is Gray."

"Oh, Gray. I'm sorry, I thought it was a telemarketer calling late."

"Did I wake you?"

"No, you didn't."

"My aunt's funeral is this Wednesday if you can make it."

"Are you sure it is okay with your mother? I don't want to cause a problem for her."

"She wants you there so she can apologize for her actions. It was the situation, not you, that upset her."

"That's perfectly understandable, no apologies necessary."

"Do you know where The Falls Church Episcopal is?"

"No, I don't but I'll find it."

"It's about fifteen miles from your apartment. The service starts at one o'clock, but the family is gathering at noon to have a private showing. We'd like you to join us and sit with the family during the service. If you text me when you're close, I'll meet you at the door."

"Oh, I can't intrude on your family's private good-bye. It wouldn't be right. I can't do that."

"Listen, everyone in the family knows about Aunt Jac

and your grandmother. They know you are Carol's granddaughter and want you with us."

"That's a very generous offer, but I'm not true family.
I will be there for the service, so I'll see you on Wednesday."

"As you wish, Livvy. Good night. Sleep well."

"Thanks, you too. Bye." I end the call and immediately call my mom.

"Well, this is a surprise. I didn't expect to hear from
you so soon."

"Mom, they want me to come to the funeral and sit
with the family. What should I do?"

"Go. You said you think that Gray is legit, so go and
maybe you will find out what Jac was all about."

"I know, but at the same time I don't want to know."

"Why?"

I snort a small laugh. "Because it means I am buying
into it all and that scares me. I mean, how is it possible that I
felt compelled to uproot myself and travel across the country
only to meet the woman my grandmother loved. Doesn't it
all seem too coincidental to you?"

"Yes it does. But, at the same time...I don't know. It
seems like predestination is playing its role for you."

"This is what is meant to be?"

"Exactly. Why not embrace it and see where it takes
you."

"I'm afraid."

"I know, sweetie. It will be a huge leap of faith on
your part, and I know you can do it. I think you should go."

I yawn. "Okay, Mom, I'll go with the flow and see
where it takes me. I knew you'd give me good advice."

"Always. Sounds like you need to go to bed so I'll
say good night."

"Okay, Mom, I'll let you know how it goes. Bye."

I stretch my arms over my head and yawn again.

Suddenly, the bed is calling my name and I am unable to resist.

†

Before I know it, Wednesday comes and I find myself on the side of the road texting Gray that I am within five minutes of arriving. I can't believe that they want me there, but I am getting the sense that my grandmother is important to them all. Why I don't know, but I hope to gather enough information to answer my questions.

I park in the lot next to the church and make my way to the entrance where I see Gray waiting for me. She is smartly dressed in a black suit, with her dark hair pulled back in a loose bun. Her face is grim, and I can see by the way she is holding her body she is tense. I square my shoulders and walk toward her.

"Right on time. I'm glad you could make it," Gray says. "Everyone is inside and waiting on us."

I reach out and touch her arm. "Please, tell me why it is so important that I be here."

Gray puts her hand over mine and squeezes it. "Patience, Livvy. I am sure you will understand once we go inside." With that, she takes my arm and walks with me into the church.

I feel my jaw drop when we enter the historic church, for it is unlike any church I've ever attended. White and light comes to mind as I view the interior. Windows line the white walls, both on the bottom and in the balcony. Behind the altar is a large window with a cross inside. I see a gathering of what I assume is Jac's family at the front of the church, and Gray guides me toward them.

A woman I now recognize as Gray's mother and Jac's younger sister, comes to me and takes my hand in both hers.

"Please, forgive me for the horrible way I treated you on Saturday. I was distraught and took it out on you and I'm sorry."

I shake my head. "No need for an apology, I didn't belong there."

"You are Carol's granddaughter, of course you belonged there. I'm so glad Jac was able to speak with you before she passed. I know her heart was heavy that she hadn't connected with you."

I don't know what to say. Apparently, this woman knows all about my grandmother, and I have no idea why she is including me. *Maybe they're all gypsies.*

"I'm Sharon Reinhart-Dawson," she says.

I frown and look at Gray. "Dawson?"

"I was young and foolish. Gray didn't want to change her name when I married ten years later."

"Oh." Two other women come up to us.

"Livvy, this is Christine, our older sister, and Dorothea our cousin."

I shake both women's hands. "Nice to meet you. I'm so sorry for your loss." I look around at Jac's family and then at the open casket.

"Come with us," Sharon says. "We are going to say our last good-byes before they close the casket."

The whole situation is so surreal that I have no other choice but to go along. I look for Gray who is staring at me intently. Sharon and the other two are in front of me, and I am glad, because that means I can't see Jac. I really don't want to see her. Then they part and one of them, Christine I think, takes my hand and urges me forward.

Jac is the first person whom I've seen dead, so I take a deep breath and look at her. She still has the same serene expression that she had when she died, and I'm wondering if this is how everyone looks when they pass. My eyes take in the whole of her and I gasp. There, around her neck is the

186

other necklace.

"She had it all along," I mumble. I recall her last words to me, "Once you find the other half you will know the love we shared." *How can that happen since Jac is wearing the necklace in her coffin?* The disappointment I feel is palpable, and I turn away only to find Gray by my side.

"Please, don't go, Livvy. It is not what it seems," she says to me.

"I don't know what kind of game you all are playing, but I don't want any part of it." I see the others looking in my direction. "What did I ever do that warranted this? God, I believed you."

"Please, stay and I will tell you everything after the burial."

I turn to leave and just as I am walking down the red-carpeted aisle, I have to step aside into a pew as what seems like a hoard of other mourners appear. I look back and see that the casket is closed and Jac's family is taking their seats. Gray is still standing and looking in my direction.

I nod in her direction remaining in the pew and taking a seat. I look in Gray's direction again and feel my heart beat a little faster.

†

Entering my apartment, I kick off my shoes and finally let my shoulders relax. The day has been emotional and at the same time interesting. I was surprised at the number of people that attended Jac's funeral. Other than Gray's family, I didn't know anyone else.

Gray made no further attempts at speaking with me, for which I was grateful. I'm not oblivious to the fact that not only Gray, but apparently her entire family thinks I'm important. For the life of me, I can't figure out why. As a tribute to my grandmother, I stayed during the church service and the burial. I chose not to attend the reception afterwards, for I was so emotionally raw that I knew any interaction with family would send me over the edge. The last thing I wanted was to let them see me cry.

My phone rings and I smile. "Hi, Mom."

"How did it go?"

"Where do I begin?"

"At the beginning." She laughs, and I can feel myself relax further.

"I love you, Mom. The day went like this…" Fifteen minutes later, I say, "So, that's why I didn't go to the meal."

"That's interesting. Do you have any thoughts as to why they treated you that way?"

"I wish I did. They acted as if I was some long lost relative who they finally found. It was so bizarre."

"From what you said, you read in the journal and letters there was a very strong bond between my mother and Jac, right?"

"Yes, and they all talked about it with such a reverence in their voices."

"And you're sure it was the same necklace?"

"Yes." I hear myself sigh. "I bought into the notion that the necklace had a special meaning, and I could kick myself for letting that happen."

"Sweetie, you told me Jac said you had to be open to the possibility that there is more that you cannot see right now. Didn't she tell you it was just waiting for you to take hold and grasp it?"

"I don't know. Yes, in a way that's what she said. Right now my mind is so frazzled that I can't think straight, much less solve the puzzle of Jac and her family." I pause. "There is something about Gray that calls to me, but I just haven't figured out what it is. Maybe the connection she has to grandmother is what I'm feeling…I want to know more."

"I know. Why don't you get a good night's sleep? It's amazing what that will do to make things clearer in the morning."

"Thanks, Mom, I'll give that a try."

"First have a glass of wine, watch an old movie, and relax."

"That sounds like a wonderful idea. I love you, Mom."

"I love you too. I'm always here if you need me."

"I know. Bye."

"Bye."

My heart is a little lighter after I end the call. Mom always has a way of grounding me. Taking her advice, I head for the kitchen to find something to eat, since I can't remember the last time I ate anything substantial.

I put my feet up on the coffee table and flick on the TV and DVD player to watch one of my all time favorite movies, *Somewhere in Time*. I have, by permission of my mom, a glass of wine and a bowl of popcorn, and I settle in to watch the romance unfold. He went back in time to find the love he lost, and I think of Jac and my grandmother's situation and hope they are together and happy at last. I doubt that I will ever experience anything close to that kind of love, even if the gypsy thinks so.

Chapter Twenty-two

While sitting at my desk, I hear a knock on the door and look up to see Bri standing there. "Can I help you?" I ask. The last thing I need right now is for Bri to be here, even if the wound of her dumping me is gone.

"How did it go yesterday?"

"It was a funeral, how do you think it went?" I give her a curious look. "How did you know?"

"The meeting for reassessment was yesterday, and you weren't there. Sally Jensen said you went to a funeral."

"Oh, right. Did I miss much?"

She approaches my desk and hands me a folder. "It's all in there. We have a meeting at nine thirty with Dr. Bogart."

"The CEO? Why?"

"Aldridge said that he's been following our progress and wants to be in on a brainstorming with the team. He indicated that this is a big deal, because in all the time he's been working here, Dr. Bogart has never asked to do this."

"In that case, I'd better read this." As Bri turns to go, I ask, "Hey, thanks for the update. How are you and Elaine working out?"

Bri smiles. "Wonderfully. I know I said it wasn't working out, but we've talked since. It's early yet, but I think she may be the *one.*"

I want to ask, *are you crazy, you just met the woman,* but say instead, "I'm happy for you." I hold up the folder. "I better get this read."

"I'll come by around quarter after nine, and we can go together."

"Great, I'd like that."

†

Dr. Bogart's office is located in the farthest corner, on the top level of the building. Adjacent to it is a conference room, which is where we meet with the CEO. Something about him seems oddly familiar and, as the meeting goes on, I realize that I saw him at Jac's funeral. *That's odd.*

I try to concentrate on the meeting while wrapping my head around the fact that he was at Jac's funeral. The meeting begins to wind down, and he tells the group that he'd like to speak one on one with a team member for an in-depth interview. The next thing I know, he is saying my name, and I look at him with what I am sure is astonishment.

"Ms. Michelson, please meet me in my office at two o'clock."

"Certainly. Do you want me to bring anything like illustrations or the prospectus we are using?"

"No, I have everything I need. I'd like to meet with everyone again next week, after you've ironed out the few problems that we found." He collects his papers. "You will all receive an interoffice memo about the date and time. Thank you for a most enlightening meeting." With that, he exits to his office.

"Wow, Livvy, that is awesome," Bri says as we leave the room.

I frown. "It's more like being sent to the principal's office. What can I possibly add that we didn't cover in the meeting?"

"From where I was sitting it looked like he kept honing in on what you had to say."

"Really? I thought it was fairly even. Everyone participated, just as we always do." I look at my wristwatch. "Are you free for lunch?" I watch as Bri looks away, and I know the answer. "Never mind. I should go over my notes before I meet with him anyway."

"Hey, I'm sorry."

"No, don't be. I can see how happy you are and it's all good. I'll catch you later." The sting of how happy she looks hurts, and I need to distance myself from her. Truth be told, yesterday was emotional enough, and I can't let myself dwell on what could have been. It's time to move on.

†

Gulping back my nervousness, I knock on Dr. Bogart's open door.

He looks up and smiles at me. "Ms. Michelson, please, come in." Once I've stepped inside, he stands and comes to greet me. "I'm very impressed by your analysis of how to restructure—"

"What is that?" *Shit I can't believe I just spoke over the CEO.* My heart is beating double-time and I feel my face heat up. "I'm so sorry. It just came out."

"What is the problem?" He doesn't seem perturbed that I interrupted him.

I point to a picture on the wall. It is one circle surrounding four entwined hearts—the exact design of my necklace.

"Oh, you mean the Anamchara symbol? For a long time, it was our symbol."

"Really? I've never seen it in the building." I can feel my inside shaking. This cannot be a coincidence.

"You haven't seen it, because the founder of our company discontinued its use almost ten years ago." He takes my arm. "Please, sit down you're white as a ghost."

I take the proffered seat while keeping my gaze on the drawing. "Who," my voice is trembling, "is the founder?" I know the answer but need to hear it from his lips.

"Jacqueline Reinhart. She left the Department of Health and Human Services with a vision that she called Anamchara."

"So, I did see you at her funeral yesterday."

"Yes, I was there. I had no idea you knew the family." He sits beside me and I look at him seeing the questions on his face.

"I recently met them. My grandmother knew Jac."

"Carol?"

I'm reeling at this revelation. "How do you know that name?"

"Jac often spoke of her and how her ideas were instrumental in the creation of Anamchara. Carol's picture was in the hall with all our board members."

"What happened to her picture? I've looked at those pictures and didn't see her there."

"When Jac resigned her position, she took the picture with her."

I make a mental note to look for Jac's picture when I leave. "What was she like to work with?"

"Jac?"

I nod.

"A delight. She had a quick mind and a keen understanding of how the social services system works." He smiled. "She always remembered everyone's birthday and made sure that they received something."

"I only met her once. I now wish I had more time with her."

He looks at me for a long moment then says, "I always sensed sadness around her, and when I'd ask if she was all right she'd say, 'nothing that dying won't cure.' When I heard of her passing, I was happy for her." He went silent. "She was my friend, and I miss her counsel and gentle way. Whether she knew it or not, my life and so many others were made better because of her."

"I'm sorry for bringing it up."

"Don't be. The memory of her will always be with me and is in Anamchara." He stood. "Now, shall we start our discussion on the model your team is devising?"

"Certainly."

†

I walk out of the building with my head spinning. Life just can't be this coincidental, yet for some reason it is. My grandmother was in love with the founder of the place where I work. When I left Dr. Bogart's office, I took the opportunity to stop and look at Jac's picture. There was no doubt that she was beautiful, but the sadness he spoke of was evident on her face.

Can love be that all consuming that it transcends time and space? Can I believe that I will ever find something close to what my grandmother and Jac had? The necklace is—my other half or so they told me—buried with the woman who loved my grandmother and is no longer a factor. Where does that leave me?

I look across the street and see the bar that my coworkers and I go to after work on Fridays. A glass of wine will help calm my nerves, and then I can figure it all out. With quick steps, I cross the street and enter Scottie's Bar.

†

"I'll have a glass of Chardonnay," I say when the waitress comes to my table.

"Aren't you here a night early?" she asks, before winking.

"Just one of those days," I say. Polly is her name and, every time I come in, she flirts with me. Maybe tonight, I'll see where it goes with her. "Doesn't look too busy, why not sit down and have a drink with me?"

"Wish I could, but the boss frowns on that." She shrugs. "But maybe, after I get off I'll join you. If you're still here that is."

"I might be able to arrange that." I need to feel and Polly just might be the release I'm looking for.

Five drinks later, I'm sure I won't be able to keep awake long enough to get together with Polly. I pick up my glass and sigh. "Life is a bitch and then you die."

"Maybe not," a voice from across the bar says. I look up expecting to see Polly and shake my head in disbelief. "What are you doing here?"

"I'm worried about you."

"Well don't be. I'm doin' just fine on my own." I know I'm slurring my words. "I need to call a cab."

"Let me take you home."

I laugh. "You're the last person I want to take me home. I'm waitin' for Polly."

"She's gone home with her boyfriend. Come on, let me take you home."

"So you can fill my head with more of your nonsense

and lies."

"I never lied to you, Livvy."

"Oh, that's right you lie by omission." My head begins to lower and the room is spinning. "Okay, you can take me, but you're not coming in…" I get up and start to fall.

Gray catches me. "I've got you."

"Why didn't you tell me she had the necklace?" I sob, as she guides me to her car.

"All is not what it seems, Livvy."

"What the hell does that mean?" I pull away from her and try to punch her arm but miss.

"Come on, let's get you home, and when you're sober, I'll answer all your questions."

"Yeah, right. So far it's questions a gazillion and answers zero." She opens the car door, and I crawl inside. Much to my chagrin, I have to let her buckle my seat belt since my hands don't want to cooperate.

†

I stumble up the sidewalk to my apartment and fumble with the key. Gray is there. She takes the key from me and opens the door.

"You've done your duty, you can go now," I say as I twist the doorknob. It doesn't open. "What's goin' on?" I shake the knob and it rattles but doesn't open.

Gray reaches in and turns the knob and it opens.

"How'd you do that?"

"Come on, let's get you settled and I'll make coffee."

"No, no, no." I waggle my finger. "You can't come in." My stomach roils, and I hold my hand over my mouth. "I think I'm going to be sick." I race inside for the bathroom, hurl myself over the toilet, and throw up. "Ugh, I hate throwing up."

"Here's a damp washcloth." Gray hands it to me and when I don't take it, she gently wipes it across my lips. "Do you think you can stand?" she asks gently.

I look at her, but she's out of focus. "Why are you here?"

"Come on, let's get you to bed." I stand and feel wobbly.

Gray wraps an arm around my waist and guides me to my bedroom.

"You gonna try to sleep with me?" I attempt to run a finger down her arm and hit only air. In my drunken haze, the thought of her making love with me is quite pleasurable. "I don't know why, but I like you," I manage to say before everything goes dark.

The next thing I know is that I'm lying in my bed, still in my clothes, with the duvet covering me. My head is pounding and my mouth tastes like someone poured vinegar in it. I swing my legs over the side of the bed and sit up. The room spins. "God, I never drink like that." I close my eyes and remember Gray bringing me home, but all I can see is the photograph of Jac on the wall at work.

It is all coming back to me; Bri's rejection, the conversation with Dr. Bogart, Jac's picture, going to the bar, Polly, and Gray. "How did she know I was there?"

Once the room stops spinning, I get up and go to the bathroom, where I vividly remember getting sick and Gray helping me. I brush my teeth and rinse with mouthwash, but the taste is still there. I have no idea what time it is, but I know I need coffee and make my way to the kitchen. It is then that I see her. Gray is curled up on my couch with the afghan my mother made me over her.

I have a flashback of her covering me with the duvet then leaning over me, tucking a strand of my blonde hair behind my ear before kissing me on the forehead. There is something else, but before it becomes clear, I see her eyes open.

"Are you awake or sleep walking?" she asks.

"I'm awake. You didn't need to stay."

"You were in a bad way and it didn't feel right leaving you alone."

"I'm making coffee. Do you want some?" I am mesmerized by the way she is stretching, and my feet won't move.

"I'd better go." I watch her get up and fold the afghan. "I think you're good on your own now."

"No," I blurt out, "don't go. I seem to remember you said you'd tell me when I was sober. As you can see I'm sober now."

She looks at her watch. "Don't you have to be at work?"

I slap my forehead. "Damn." After what I learned from Dr. Bogart, I am more confused than ever, and Gray is the only one who may have the answers. "Okay, I get off at four. Will you meet me back here at four thirty? Please?"

"Are you sure that is what you want?" There is a cautious tone to her voice and that is unusual.

"I need to know everything, Gray, and you are the only one who knows *everything*."

"Well, we gypsies do have a way of seeing things." She grins. "I will be here on one condition."

"And that is?"

"That we go to dinner first. My treat."

I consider her words, trying to figure out if she has an ulterior motive or not. *She always does.* "What the hell, why not?"

"You barely have enough time to get ready for work and be there on time. The last time you ate anything substantial was yesterday morning. Go get ready for work, and I'll make you a breakfast sandwich you can eat on the way."

"I don't need you to do that."

"I know, but I'm going to do it anyway. You usually don't stop for lunch and you need something to keep you going so you can be productive."

I can feel her green eyes penetrating me as if she is seeing into my soul. "You don't know that."

"Gypsies know things like that. Now go shower."

"What if I don't want to?" I know I sound like a petulant child, but I can't help myself.

An eyebrow raise is my answer.

"Okay, I'll go, and as for dinner, I'll pay my own way."

When I am dressed and come out of the bedroom, Gray is there with the promised breakfast, a hard egg sandwich. "Thank you."

"You're welcome." She shrugs. "I'll see you back here at four thirty then."

"Okay." I watch as she makes her way to the door and lets herself out. Bizarre is the only word I can think of to describe how I'm feeling. It is like nothing I've ever felt before. As hard as I try to make sense out of my mixed up emotions, everything seems so jumbled that I doubt I will ever be able to unravel it all. One thing I know for sure—I'm looking forward to seeing Gray again.

Chapter Twenty-three

TGIF goes through my mind, as the day seems to drag on forever. I look at my phone and see it is only eleven thirty.

Bri appears at my door smiling. "Hey, you up for lunch?"

I look at her and frown. "Why do you want to have lunch with me? Where's Elaine?"

"I miss having lunch with you," she says. "As for Elaine, it turns out she has a girlfriend she neglected to mention."

"Oh. I bet that was awkward."

"To say the least. So, what about lunch?"

"Not today. Since I was out Wednesday, I'm playing catch up." Truth is that I'm feeling the residual effects of my over indulgence last night. The breakfast Gray made for me was delicious but is now churning in my stomach, and the last thing I want is more to eat.

"Right. Well, what about dinner? I really miss you."

Sure she does, until someone else comes along. I guess she really takes friends with benefits to heart. "Sorry, I have a date." It feels good to say that.

"Anyone I know?"

"Not unless you know someone named Grayson."

"Nope. Where'd you meet?"

My phone rings. "I've got to take this. I'll catch up with you later." She shrugs and leaves. "Hello, this is Livvy Michelson."

†

I work through lunch and leave for the day at three thirty. I'm anxious to get home, take a shower, and find just the right outfit to wear on my 'date' with Gray. I think that Gray is sophisticated, since every time I see her she always looks perfectly put together. The problem is I don't know what I have that meets that definition. Stylish has never been in my vocabulary.

I pull out my black slacks, a pink silk blouse, and a black blazer. For a moment, I think about Jac and conclude that Gray probably dresses similar to the way she did. Looking in the mirror, I am happy with how I look and walk out of the bedroom to wait for Gray's arrival.

The knock on the door makes my stomach quiver, and I know it is because it is Gray knocking. Taking a deep breath, I go to the door, open it, and have to catch my breath. Gray looks amazing. She's wearing a black dress with a plunging neckline that gives a glimpse of her breast. Over that is a white bolero jacket that fits her perfectly. My eyes take in every inch of her and I am speechless.

"Can I come in?" She's grinning.

I shake my head. "Yeah, sure. You look fantastic," I gush and don't know where it is coming from.

"You look pretty hot yourself. Are you ready to go?"

"Let me get my bag." I pick it up off the table next to

201

the door. "Where are you taking me?"

"Deux Amants. It's a small, out of the way French restaurant near Tyson's Corner. I hope you'll like it."

"I'm sure I will. Let's go."

†

I shiver when Gray puts her hand in the small of my back as we enter the restaurant. The maître d` addresses Gray by name and expresses his sympathies for her loss. They exchange quiet words, before he gestures for us to follow him.

Our table is in a secluded alcove, and the word intimate immediately comes to mind. As we walk through the small dining area, I can see the strong French accent with elegant appointments in the wall decorations.

"Do you come here often?" I ask.

"This was a favorite of Jac's. She brought me here ten years ago and told me that the only other person she'd ever brought here was your grandmother. When Jac became ill, I began bringing her here once a month." Sadness crosses her face. "She said it gave her comfort, and I believe it did. On those days, she always would take a turn for the better."

"I can see the appeal. This place has an ambience of peace and comfort and..." I look at her and bite my lip. "Do you come here with dates often?" Even though I don't consider this a date but more of a fact finding mission, for some reason, her answer is important to me. I hold my breath in anticipation.

"No. Other than my aunt, you are the only person I've shared it with."

My body starts to tingle. "Tell me about the necklace."

At that moment, the server appears. "Would you like the usual wine?" she asks.

"Yes, and we will have the Brie with fresh fruit as a starter." Once the server leaves, Gray looks at me. "I hope you don't mind my ordering for us."

"No. If the meal we had when we first met is any indication, I will like everything you order."

Gray looks away, and I can see a blush rise up her neck. "Thank you. Please excuse me for a minute."

I watch as she walks back the way we came and am curious about her abrupt departure. So far, Gray has been somewhat reticent, and I find that in contradiction to the person I've met in the past. Clearly distraught when speaking of Jac, I decide not to ask her anymore questions. Instead, I just enjoy the ambience of this wonderful restaurant and Gray's company.

"Sorry about that." Gray sits back down. "I spoke with the chef, and he is going to make us a special, classic French meal."

"I like the sound of that. I've never really eaten much in the way of French cuisine, so I'm looking forward to it." She seems pleased with my words. I forge ahead. "Do you live in DC permanently?"

"I did. Now, I live about twenty minutes from here."

"Why the change?"

"I've inherited Jac's home."

Just then, our appetizer arrives and we begin our French feast. Our conversation while eating is relaxed, and Gray is a wonderful dinner companion. The meal consists of frogs' legs, duck foie gras, crème brûlée, crayfish gratin with wild mushrooms, and potatoes dauphinoise. The meal ends with Galettete Pérougienne, which is a brioche-dough tart topped with whipped cream and fresh strawberries.

"I visited Pérouges, a small medieval town outside of Lyon in France, and this is the exact meal we had there." Her face is beaming. "Jac and I went there yearly until she got sick. She said she missed the dessert, so I found the recipe and started to make it for her." She looks at me, and I see tears brimming in her eyes. "I miss her so. She was like a second mother to me."

I reach across the table and take her hand. "I wish I had more time with her. I feel as though I lost someone special that I never got a chance to know better, like my grandmother."

"Once I found you, I suggested that you two meet, but she was so sick and frail that just the mention of you sent her into a tail spin. I think she knew her time had come to an end that is why she consented to finally see you."

"I don't understand."

"You know about the confrontation she had with your mother right?"

I nod.

"She was afraid you felt the same way."

I close my eyes and feel my heart breaking, realizing that actions of the past can have dire ramifications on the present. A tear trickles down my cheek and I wipe it away. "I'm so sorry."

Gray squeezes my hand. "In the end, you and she connected, and that is all that matters." She lets go and pushes back her chair. "Are you ready to leave?"

I look at Gray and a feeling of warmth and caring fills me. *When did that happen?* "Okay, but I have to warn you that with all the food I ate, I might be slow."

"Not a problem, I'll stay with you."

"I'm counting on it." My heart begins beating wildly at all the possibilities of what I am feeling for Gray. "Back to my place?" I give her a wink and head for the door.

Chapter Twenty-four

I look at Gray as we get out of her car and head for my apartment. Her beautiful face is drawn, and I can see what I think looks like regret. "Are you okay?" I ask, as I unlock the door.

We step inside, she takes my hand, and in that instant, I feel an affinity with her that seems so right. "It hasn't even been a week. You must be an emotional wreck. Has she spoken with you?"

Gray shakes her head and I hear her sigh. "She came to me the night she passed and told me she was truly happy. You see, only souls that are troubled speak to me, so I know that I'll never connect with her again."

I instinctively pull her into my arms and hold her close, feeling her trembling body next to mine. We stay like that for a long moment before she takes a step away. "Don't shut me out, Gray. I know I wasn't your biggest fan when we first met, but things change and I'm here for you."

"I can't do this right now," she says and moves farther away.

I am determined not to let her get away. "Not a problem. I have the time to wait." I look directly into her eyes. "I'm not going anywhere, because I understand now about being open to the possibilities."

Sometime in the last hours, I'd come to the realization that what I was looking for was right in front of me. I know that for some time now I've been thinking of Gray differently. I just was too self-absorbed to see it. I can feel a connection between the lives of my grandmother, Jac, Gray, and me, just as the one circle surrounds the four intertwined hearts of the necklace. I shiver at the rightness of it all.

"Why don't you go home and, when you're ready, call me. We can have a frank conversation about our unique situation."

"I'm not sure when that will happen." She shrugs. "I'm too shattered right now for anything that intense." She closes her eyes and lets out a small sigh.

"I understand." I give her a hug. "Do you think you'd be up for a road trip tomorrow?"

She looks at me and her brow furrows. "What do you have in mind?"

"One of the places I've always wanted to visit is the Philadelphia Museum of Art. I was planning to go by myself tomorrow but would love it if you joined me."

"You know that on a good day that is at least a three-hour trip just to get there."

"I know. I've been researching the trip for weeks now. It opens at ten, so if we leave no later than six we can have time for breakfast on the way and still be there when they open." I look at her and smile. "What do you say? Are you up for it?"

Gray blows out a breath. "Normally, I avoid museums, because they are full of lost souls."

"Oh, I hadn't thought of that. I guess that applies to all museums then, huh."

"It is a hazard of my profession but one I can control, so if you want to go to Philly, we can go."

"Really?" I hug her again and this time I don't let go. "Going with you will be fantastic."

She takes a step back and I feel bereft.

"I'll be by to pick you up at six and bring breakfast with me," she says.

"I can drive. You are stressed and might need to just sit and watch the road go by."

"Driving relaxes me, so I'll drive."

"Okay. Are you going to bring one of those yummy egg sandwiches you made for me the last time?"

Her smile is genuine. "Of course."

"It's a date then."

"Yes, it is." She looks uncharacteristically nervous. "I guess I'll go now and see you in the morning."

I go to her and give her a chaste kiss on the lips. "Yes, you will." When the door closes behind her, I lean against it, my heart racing. "I have a date with Gray Reinhart."

†

The next morning, I am up at five. After my shower, I begin sorting through all my clothes, discarding one outfit after another, finally deciding on skinny jeans and a long-sleeve, blue J Crew chambray shirt over a white camisole. I finished the outfit off with a pair of tall boots. When I look in the mirror, I take it all off and start again. When Gray arrives, I have on a pair of jeans, a Henley shirt, Reebok Crossfit shoes, and a light jacket.

I open the door and grin. Gray is wearing an outfit similar to the first one I tried on. "You look great."

"You're not so bad yourself." Gray holds up a bag. "Do you want to eat this here or in the car?"

"I am so excited about going, do you mind if we eat on the way?"

"Not at all. I know there is a Starbucks along the way, and I thought we could stop there for coffee."

"Sounds like a plan." I collect my keys and wallet before locking the door and following Gray to her car.

†

At this time of the morning, Highway 95 is not very congested and Gray merges her Mercedes into the traffic with ease. Once we are in the flow of the traffic, I put her cup of coffee in a cup holder before pulling out one of the sandwiches, unwrapping it, and handing it to her.

"Thanks."

I watch as she keeps her eyes on the road while taking a bite. It isn't the first time I notice my body's reaction to how attractive she is, but it is the most profound. I shake away the thought and bite into my sandwich. "This is really good. Are you a chef in disguise?"

Gray smiles. "I admit I do like to cook, although I rarely have the time to do much of it."

"You're that busy?"

"You'd be surprised at the number of people who want to connect with a dearly departed. I get around a hundred emails a day from people wanting a consultation."

"Do you answer them all? That must be overwhelming to keep up with."

"Yes. At one time I had an assistant who helped, but I soon realized it was a shortcut and defeated the purpose of what I was doing." She lifts one shoulder. "It is something only I can do."

Digesting her words, I find myself more enamored with her than ever before. "That's admirable of you." I sigh.

"I'm sorry I ever doubted you." I put my sandwich down and look out the window, not wanting to show my embarrassment at how I treated her in the past.

"Livvy," her voice is soft, "in the end you understood and that is all that matters to me. This connection we have was always there and although I saw it, you needed time to realize its importance."

I reach out and touch her arm. "I think I knew from the start and that is why I was so set against you."

Gray grins. "I know."

I playfully slap her arm. "No, you didn't."

"Gypsies know all."

We arrive at the museum just after ten, and Gray takes my hand and leads me to the east entrance of the museum to see the statue of Rocky and the infamous steps.

"Wow." I look down the expansive stairs that herald the flag-lined Benjamin Franklin Parkway. "We should have come for the weekend. This is fantastic."

"When I was twelve, my family, along with my grandparents and Aunt Jac, came here to visit. The statue wasn't here then. When I heard about it becoming a permanent fixture, I wanted to come see it but never made the time." She hugs me. "Thank you for this," she whispers.

I smile and hug her back. "Thank you for coming with me. Let's go. I hear a van Gogh calling my name."

We took a half hour to eat lunch in the museum's restaurant before exploring more of the art. By closing time, we still hadn't seen all the museum had to offer. Walking out the main entrance, we begin taking a circuitous route around the museum to where the car is parked. "You were right," Gray says. "we should have planned on spending the weekend."

"We still can. All we need to do is buy some clothes and a toothbrush and we'd be set. I don't think we will have any trouble finding a hotel room either. It is Philadelphia, after all."

Gray sighs. "As delightful as that sounds, my family is having a get-together to honor Jac tomorrow, and I have to be there."

"You know, I am disappointed, because I really like spending time with you, but I know how important that is to you. We can do it another time then. We have the rest of our lives."

We arrive at her car. "Hey, why don't you come with me? I know they'd all like to see you again." Gray takes my hand. "Please."

I get in shaking my head. "I don't get why your family seemed so enamored with me. It was not only disconcerting but embarrassing since they didn't know me from Adam."

Gray didn't start the car. "You have to understand that until Jac met your grandmother she wasn't a very nice person. She used people and generally treated them with disdain. Of course, to the world she was charming, but to her family she was horrible. She changed completely after meeting Carol. Even though they never met her, she was welcomed as one of us."

"But I'm not her."

She takes my hand. "You are part of her and to my family that is everything."

"Is it okay if I think that odd?"

Gray smiles. "Of course it is. Will you come with me?"

"Yes."

She starts the car and begins to back out, only to stop. "I don't know about you, but that quiche we had at the museum restaurant has long left my stomach."

As if on cue, my stomach rumbles and I laugh. "I think food is in order. Never had one but I hear Pat's cheesesteak is the best there is."

"Great idea. I'll put it in the nav system."

I feel my mouth water as I think of eating a cheesesteak. The upside is I can prolong the day with Gray. The prospect of spending Sunday with her family is daunting, but if it means I can be with her I will gladly go.

Chapter Twenty-five

I fidget with my seat belt as I look at the house where Gray's family is gathered. I cannot believe that I agreed to be here, but it gives me another opportunity to be with Gray and that is a definite plus. In a way, I don't want Gray to think I'm muscling in on her family at this stage of our relationship. Some might think that. I can't afford to make that mistake. Gray is my future. I know it in every fiber of my being.

When she arrives at my apartment this morning she looks so cute. She hold out a Starbucks cup containing my favorite Peppermint White Chocolate Mocha.

"You remembered," I say, as I eagerly took the offered cup.

She tapped her forehead. "Mind like a steel trap." She gave me a quick hug. "Are you ready to go? They start brunch promptly at ten thirty."

Now, I am walking up the sidewalk toward a door where, once inside, I will meet with Gray's entire family, or at least the closest members. If the number of cars parked along the street is any indication, there will be a lot of people behind the door. Gray takes my hand, and I feel my body react as tingles shoot through me.

"Stop worrying. They are looking forward to you joining the family."

I laugh. "I feel like you are bringing me home to meet the folks." *Am I reading too much into her words "joining the family?"* God, I hope not. I guess I'll find out soon enough.

"You've already met most of them at Jac's funeral." Gray reaches for the doorknob. "You ready?"

"As ready as I'll ever be."

It's probably my imagination, but it seems to me that a hush fills the house when we step inside. I look around and the number of cars outside does not match the number of people I see. "Wow." Gray squeezes my hand and I relax. "Are all these people relatives of yours?"

"Yes. We meet like this once every six months. My grandparents started the tradition twenty years ago."

Sharon, Gray's mother, comes up to me. "Livvy, I'm so glad you could join us." She takes my arm. "Come with me and meet the family properly this time."

Panic fills me, and I look at Gray who grins and leans into me. "You can do it, they don't bite," she whispers. Sharon begins to whisk me away, and I grab Gray's hand. There's no way I'm meeting the family without her by my side.

The meet and greet with Sharon doesn't last long. A tall woman with silver hair that I recognize as Christine, Jac's older sister, raises her hand in the air. As if on cue, everyone stops and looks in her direction.

"We are blessed by being together as a family again," Christine says. "It is with great sadness that we have lost one of our own." She raises a glass.

I see everyone do the same. Sharon hands me a glass with what looks like some sort of punch.

"To Jac," Christine says, and a hum of "to Jac" fills the room.

I look at Gray and see a profound sadness on her face. My heart goes out to her, and I move closer and put my hand in hers. She looks at me, closes her eyes briefly, then mouths, *thanks*.

While Gray and I are sitting on a couch eating, Christine approaches us. "Livvy, it is so good to see you again."

"You too Mrs. Mitchell."

She looks at Gray. "How are the renovations going?"

"Everything should be completed by the end of next week. They are putting the finishing touches on the kitchen."

"You will be nearby at last."

"Yes. I'm looking forward to it." Gray looks at me. "Would you like to go see where I'll be living before I take you home?"

Christine laughs. "Now that's an offer any girl should be scared of. Gray, Reece needs a quick word."

I recognize the name as Christine's son.

She waves over a man I haven't met before. He looks scholarly in a comfortable kind of way. His thick rimmed glasses make him look like he's seeing out of jam jars. His well-worn sweater looks out of place with the majority of the folks in the room. My first thought as he shyly smiles at me is that he's adorable in a benign way.

"Christine, how can I help you?"

Gray hugs him close.

"Dad," I see her narrow her eyes. "Mom told me you were playing chess with Cuthbert in memory of Jac. Did he bail?"

The bald head shakes vigorously. "Nope, he's in the study, I needed a drink."

Gray laughs and looks at me. "Dad, this is Livvy."

So this is her step-father. I don't recall seeing him at

the funeral.

"Will you keep her company for a few minutes while I have a quick chat with Reece, please?" Gray winks in my direction and then kisses her father's cheek before heading into the throng of people.

For all of two minutes, I am uncomfortable until Gray's dad speaks.

"It's a bit intimidating, this whole family get-together thing, don't you think?"

I nod and then whisper, "Yes."

He places a knurled hand on my forearm and chuckles. "If you want to be with Gray, get used to this. I know I had to."

"Well I...I mean, she's a friend. We haven't known each other that long." I can feel my forehead furrow.

"Now, don't go marking that pretty face of yours with frowns. Sharon hates her frown lines and detests the laughter ones even more—there are more of them, you see. I just say that's having a good life and accept it. You women have a different mantra to that kind of thing, I've found."

I smile. Gray's dad is nice, ordinarily nice, and it is comforting. I don't feel like an outsider around him. "Thank you."

He squeezes my arm gently. "You are an important new member of my family, and I will look after you. I'd be a terrible parent otherwise."

His statement floors me, and I wonder if there is a connection with the entire family to another dimension in their acceptance of everything and everyone? That notion blows my mind.

A hand descends on my shoulder, and instinctively I know the owner. I smile, thinking that I must be channeling their mind-set. "That was quick."

Gray grins. "For you, of course. Dad, Mom asks if

you are interested in leaving now and having Italian for dinner?"

He has a huge grin and answers with an enthusiastic yes.

Gray's dad turns to me. "Do you like Italian food?" I nod.

He turns to Gray. "Dinner at our place in two weeks. You can bring Italian from Tony's." He smiles at me. "If you will excuse me," he says before heading into the morass of people.

My eyes are on Gray's dad leaving, but my ears were waiting for Gray's reaction.

She doesn't say anything but looks at me. "You never replied if you wanted to see my new place?"

"I'd love to." We make our rounds, saying good-bye to everyone before leaving.

†

When we pull into the driveway, I see the most beautiful Tudor-style home with a huge front porch. "Oh, Gray, what a wonderful home."

Gray sighs. "It is filled with memories of growing up and visiting Jac here." Her eyes fill with tears. "I keep thinking she will appear, but I know better."

I place my hand over her heart. "She's in here, isn't she?"

"Yes." Gray pulls me to her. "She brought me you." Taking a step back, she smiles. "Come on, I want to show you the kitchen."

"This is fantastic. It looks like a high-end kitchen for a chef."

Gray grins. "In another life, I'm sure I must have been. Now, I can cook to my heart's delight." She puts her arm around my waist. "I'd like to cook for you."

"I normally cook for others, so yes, absolutely yes."

"Good answer."

When Gray's lips caress mine, I melt into them. I run my tongue over her lips and she responds. Just as the kiss is deepening, her phone rings and she pulls away.

"Really? Please don't answer," I say.

"That ring tone means it is business. Hold that thought for one minute okay?"

I nod.

"This is Natasha Gabor."

I watch, as the expression on her face grows somber. The person speaking has her full attention and, for a moment, I'm forgotten. She looks at her wrist watch.

"Yes, I will arrange for a private jet immediately, and be there as soon as I can." Gray ends the call. "I'm needed in Colorado." She punches in a number on her phone. "Josh, it's Natasha. I need to be in the air for Colorado immediately. Can you arrange that?" She nods. "Good. I will be there within the hour." Gray ends the call.

"Is it serious?"

"Yes, very. I'm sorry to cut this short."

"Can I say I'm not happy but understand?" I smile at her.

I see the crinkle around her eyes as she smiles—it's genuine. "Yes. I'll drop you off on my way to the private air-field."

"Don't you need to pack?"

"I always have a 'go bag' in my trunk."

†

"I'm not sure how long I'll be gone." Gray says, as she stops in front of my apartment.

"I'll still be here." I move closer to her and kiss her cheek. "You have my number. Call it." Her lips are so close to mine that I move away from the temptation.

"I will. I promise." She gives me a hug and lingers for a moment before she kisses my lips.

I lean into her and when she pulls away, I feel bereft. "Be safe and come back to me."

"I will." With that, she is gone, and I stand stock still watching her car disappear down the street.

†

Two hours later, I am sitting on the couch eating ice cream trying to get my head around my feelings for Gray. Everything about the weekend with her invades my every thought. Friday night was fabulous. It was touching that she had the chef prepare a special meal just for me.

Saturday, at the art museum, was one of those days that I will always remember. Gray was so open and animated that at times she astounded me. Sunday with her family gave me insight into who she is. I knew then that I want her in my life.

My phone rings and I smile. "Hey."

"Hi."

When I hear Gray's voice, I feel a goofy smile form on my lips. "Hi. Did you miss your flight?"

"No, I'm in the air now. I'm sorry I had to leave in such a hurry, Livvy. I promised to answer your questions this weekend and didn't. You deserve to have answers."

"I know you will when you can."

"I land in a little while, so I'll give you the condensed version for now."

"It doesn't have to be now, Gray. It can wait."

"No, I want to tell you. The simplest explanation is

that love transcends many lifetimes."

I close my eyes and the sound of her voice soothes me.

"The one thing Jac kept telling me about your grandmother was that she said these words. 'If we ignore what has happened in the past, we never will recognize what is familiar about now...' She would tell me that to ignore the past is to ignore all that you are."

"That sounds profound but oddly true."

"The fact is that when I died and Jac brought me back to life, our souls joined. I am a part of her for all time."

"Just like I am with my grandmother?" My eyes open in understanding of the rightness of those words.

"Exactly."

"Then what does it all mean?" I look at the melting ice cream.

"That two souls joined are bound together for all eternity."

"More puzzles, Gray?"

"Unfortunately, yes. When I return from my trip, can we solve that puzzle together?"

"I'd like that."

"Me too."

"Don't forget to call me when you get to Colorado so I know you're okay."

"I will try. Sometimes, the moment I step off the plane I am immediately engaged in whatever the mystery is."

"Okay, Gray. Be safe."

"Thank you. Good-bye, Livvy, sweet dreams."

Chapter Twenty-six

Monday, I feel like a caged animal as I pace around my apartment. My mind was so scattered when I woke that I took the day off. Except for the call from the plane, I haven't heard from Gray and she promised she'd let me know when she arrived. I'm worried about her, especially since I've seen the news coming out of Colorado. She hasn't answered any of my calls. Twice, I called my work number to make sure my phone was working—it was. No matter how I try to distract myself, she keeps invading my thoughts. Jac's voice saying "all you have to do, my sweet girl, is be open to the possibility" won't stop.

"Why aren't you calling me? Maybe just speaking to someone who cares about you might help." I look at the story again and silently pray that Gray will be okay.

I turn on the TV and start flicking through the channels until I see the story again about a six-year-old girl missing in Colorado. The police spokesperson is telling the reporters that they are pursuing every avenue. "Some are conventional, others are not," she says. I immediately think of Gray. I open my laptop, and search for *child missing in Colorado*. I don't find any reference to Gray, but in one grainy photo, I think I see her in the crowd.

I take out my phone and text her. *Saw the news. Are you okay?*

Five minutes later, I get a response. *Very intense, sorry can't talk.*

With a sigh of relief, I text *K*. At least I know she isn't avoiding me.

Suddenly exhausted and feeling drained, I head for my bed. Crawling under the covers, I close my eyes and instantly I see Gray. I let my mind go with the image. I remember Gray tucking me in when I was drunk and leaning over me, kissing my forehead. My eyes fly open. "She was wearing the other necklace!" I wrack my brain to remember if she had it on when we went to dinner. I remember the neckline of her dress and can see a gold chain disappearing under the dress. I then remember seeing the same chain when I first met her.

"I should have known it was her." I yawn and close my eyes. Soon, I can feel sleep taking me into its arms.

✝

I'm sitting at my desk the next day, when Bri walks into my office.

"How was your date?"

She stands next to me like she used to when we were friends with benefits, and I smell the familiar perfume. "Please, don't stand there like that. The door is open."

"It never bothered you before." She doesn't move.

"That was before you found someone else."

"I was afraid of my feelings for you. After Sara, I promised myself to never let myself fall again."

"Huh. I thought you said what's-her-name is *the one*."

"I made a mistake. Will you forgive me and give me another try?"

"I'll forgive you, but can't give you another try, Bri, because I can't trust you not to do it again."

"Please? Can we have a real loving partnership instead of what we had?"

I hear the desperation behind her voice and hate to see her grovel. "No."

Bri smiles and lets out a breath. "Are you sure we can't try again?"

My cell rings and I look at the read out. Gray. "Hi, can you hold on for a minute... Great." I look at Bri. "I have to take this."

"Okay. Can we have lunch?"

"Not today. Some other time."

She nods and leaves closing the door behind her.

"Gray, are you back? I've missed you."

"No. I'm about to board the plane." Her voice sounds flat.

"What airport?"

"Dulles."

"What's your flight number? I'll pick you up."

"I've already arranged for a car to pick me up to take me to my suite at the Monaco."

"Oh. Okay." I feel my heart go from in the clouds ecstatic to tumbling down to earth.

"Livvy, it's not you. I need a few days to decompress. Cases involving kids are always the most stressful."

My heart goes out to her, and all I want to do is hold her and comfort her. "I could hold you and help ease your pain."

"I appreciate that, Livvy, but I'm in a dark place right now, and I won't be fit to be around. Please, understand."

222

"I do. Remember that I am here for you any time day or night."

"You figured it out didn't you?" she says.

"Yes. I remembered seeing the necklace you were wearing the night I was drunk and you brought me home. After that, everything just fell into place. Now, I can't wait to explore all the possibilities open to us."

"Me too. Look, they are boarding, so I have to go. I'll call you in a few days when I'm in a better frame of mind."

"Okay. Be safe." I hear the phone go silent, and I know she is gone. A plan begins to percolate. "First, I'll need to talk with Aldridge."

†

I speak with Aldridge, telling him I have a family emergency and I need to be gone for the rest of the week. It isn't really a lie. My grandmother, Jac, Gray, and me have a deep connection and isn't that the definition of family?

A quick search of the internet lets me know that the travel time from Denver to DC is around three and a half hours. I will need to make a reservation at the Hotel Monaco, go home and pack a bag, and then drive to DC. It is doable, if I don't waste any time.

First, I call the hotel and hold my breath that a room is available. It is. Then I make sure all my data is up-to-date and send it to the team leader, explaining that I will be unavailable until the following week. With everything in order, I leave work and head home to take a quick shower and pack a bag.

†

It is early evening when I finally arrive at the hotel. An accident snarled traffic, making me about an hour behind schedule.

Entering the lobby, I go straight to the check-in counter and get my room number. I smile at the woman helping me. "I hope you can help me."

"I'll try."

"Great. I'm supposed to meet with Grayson Reinhart, and I'm running behind. Do you know if she's arrived yet?"

"Yes. I saw her come in about an hour or so ago. Would you like me to ring her room for you?"

"No. I need to settle into my room first. I'll just call her suite after that. Thank you." I walk quickly to the elevator, anxious to get to my room so I can deposit my bag before going to Gray's room. I know I am taking a big chance and that there is every possibility that Gray will refuse to see me, but the reward is too great not to go forward with my plan.

I can feel my body quivering, as I stand in front of Gray's door. I take a deep breath to settle my nerves, then knock softly and wait.

Nothing.

I knock harder. When there still isn't an answer, I decide to go back to my room and try again later. *Maybe she's taking a shower.* Just as I turn away, I hear the chain on the door moving and swallow hard. *This is it.* I know now that I've been waiting for this moment ever since I first met her. Gray is where I belong.

When the door opens, my heart goes out to her. Her face, much as it looked at Jac's funeral, is creased and drawn. "Oh, sweetheart, look at you." I move inside the room and take her in my arms. She leans into me and begins to cry. In the background, I hear the ping of the elevator and push the door closed with my foot.

I stand there with her in my arms running a hand up and down her back. "It's going to be okay. I've got you and I won't let you fall." When I pull back, I caress her face and wipe the tears away with my thumb. "Let's sit down," I say softly and she nods. Taking her hand, I lead her to the sofa and when we sit, I am right next to her.

"Tell me," I say.

For a long moment, she says nothing. In a broken voice she finally says, "As soon as I went to the place where she was last seen, I could hear her crying—wailing is more like it. She was lost, hurt, and wanted her mommy. I knew since I could hear her that she was gone. Her desperate parents began peppering me with questions, and I couldn't bring myself to tell them that I knew that their child was gone." Gray begins to weep softly. "I followed her voice and when they finally found her she was at the bottom of a ravine."

Gray wipes her hand over her face. "I can't get the image of her broken body out of my head. She was only six years old, with white-blonde hair. When I speak to the dead, I don't see the person I only hear their voice. Except..."

"When Jac passed," I say.

"Yes." She begins to shake. "Oh, God, it was so horrible."

I tighten my grip on her, and she rests her head on my shoulder. Her body convulses while she cries. Eventually, she relaxes and her sobs subside.

"Why are you here?" she asks.

"You needed me. I couldn't stay away."

"But I told you—"

I put a finger over her lips. "You needed me." In the deepest recesses of my soul, I know the truth of those three words. "You will never again have to go to that dark place alone."

"Thank you." She places her forehead on mine. "I've waited so long for you." She kisses me so softly, I'm not sure it is real. "I need to get some sleep. Will you stay with me?"

"Yes, I will hold you and keep you safe all night. I'll even chase away the demons." I stand and hold out my hand. She takes it, and we walk hand in hand into the bedroom.

The second that her head hits the pillow, Gray is asleep. At first, she is fitful but after I wrap her in my arms, she settles down and sighs in what sounds like contentment. I look at her beautiful face and sigh myself. I know that she is the reason I journeyed across the country and began working at Anamchara. It is as it should be. When I pull the sheet over her, I see the necklace lying on her chest. I close my eyes, as warmth and love spread throughout my body. Our being together was preordained before either of us was born. I am hers and she is mine for all time. With that joyous thought, I close my eyes and let sleep take me too.

Chapter Twenty-seven

I wake up to find myself alone in Gray's bed. The sheet is still warm, and I surmise she hasn't been gone long. The clothes that I wore the day before are still on, and I desperately want to change them. If I go to my room and get my suitcase, will she let me stay? Did I overstep the boundaries by showing up at her door unannounced? I can't screw this up. Not now. Not since I found the one person, I've been unknowingly searching for all my life.

I hear the bathroom door open and look to see Gray wearing a white robe with a towel wrapped around her head. She smiles at me and my heart soars. "Good morning," I say. "How are you feeling this morning?"

"Better, thanks to you." She comes to the bed and sits down. "In the past, Jac always comforted me and the thought of her not being here along with the emotional events in Denver were overwhelming." She smiles. "Then you showed up and took me in your arms and helped me through the night by lifting the burden off my heart. Thank you." She strokes my cheek. "It was more than I could take, and I was crashing as I never have before. I needed you. I've always needed you."

"Did you always know it was me?"

"A year after I was struck by lightning, Jac came to me and told me that I was saved because I had great things left to do in my life. She gave me the necklace and told me that the other half of my soul was waiting for me. Find the other necklace." Gray sucks in a breath. "I didn't know it was you until the moment I first saw you." With a lift of one shoulder she says, "Suddenly, everything fell into place and I knew it was you I'd been looking for."

"I thought you were a charlatan."

She laughs. "I know. A gypsy, I think it was."

"It is strange how it all came together. I mean my coming to work at Anamchara, meeting Bri, her knowing you, going to your event," I shake my head, "if it all hadn't happened as it did, we never would have met."

"Have you ever come upon an accident on the road that has just occurred?" Gray asks.

"Yes."

"Did you ever think that if you had been a few seconds earlier, it might have been you?"

"Of course, doesn't everyone?"

"No, but that's not the point. Everything in the universe works exactly as it should. You were never going to be in the accident."

"You mean it is preordained?"

"Exactly. This may seem strange but when I got Briana's first mail, I knew that she was somehow connected to finding you."

"Wow. You know that as hard as I tried, I couldn't deny you. I kept running you down in my mind, but I think that something inside my heart recognized you, because my mind kept coming back to you. I chose to ignore it when I got involved with Bri." I look at her. "I guess we have to go places we don't belong before we can find where we do. Does that make any sense to you?"

"Perfect sense. For a long time, I'd bed women thinking that surely, I'd find the one. Then Jac told me about your grandmother and told me it would be worth the wait. Now that I'm sitting here with you, even though we've only kissed, I know she was right."

I place my hand over my heart. "In here, I know that to be true."

Gray gives me a curious look.

"What?"

"You're still in the same clothes. Sorry if I kept you from going home last night, but I am glad you stayed."

"You didn't. I have a room in the hotel."

"You do? Why?"

"I was prepared to stay here for as long as it took to get through to you." I look down at my rumpled clothes. "Why don't I go change and then we can have breakfast together."

"I have a better idea." Gray winked. "Why don't you check out and bring your bag here. You can stay with me if you'd like." Her words sound tentative.

"Well, I do have the rest of the week off."

"Then you'll do it?"

"Yes. I'll go get a quick shower, change my clothes, and be back in, say, forty minutes."

"I'll order breakfast. What would you like?"

"What would you suggest?"

"I'm particularly fond of the eggs benedict with a side of fresh fruit." She looks at me. "They put a marvelous honey-vanilla Greek yogurt over the fruit."

"Sounds yummy." I move to her and kiss her lips and she responds. Her lips are soft and supple, and I know if I don't stop, my hands will find their way inside her robe. I pull back. "To be continued, so keep that in mind while I'm gone."

"Tease."

I grin. "Trust me, waiting will be worth it."

"I'm counting on it."

"Right, I better go. I'll be back." I reluctantly leave the bedroom and head for the door. It'll be a record-setting shower, of that I'm sure.

†

Gray opens the door and I roll my suitcase inside. I give her a hasty kiss and say, "I'll go check out and be right back."

"Already done."

"I can pay for my own room."

"I know you can. Being a semi-permanent resident has its benefits, and I was able to get your room comped. Besides," she grins, "now we have more time to be together."

"I like the sound of that." I move to her and take her in my arms. "I have plans for you, so I hope you haven't ordered breakfast yet." There is a light knock on the door and I step back.

Gray shrugs. "Sorry, I can send it away."

"No, I'm starving." I'm starving for more than food, but I've waited this long, and I have a feeling we will both need the nourishment.

Once Gray shuts the door after the woman who delivers our breakfast leaves, she comes to me and kisses me lightly. "While you were gone, I had an idea."

"Really? What was that?"

"A leisurely breakfast followed by this," she kisses me, "and this," she runs her fingers down my body. "What do you think?"

230

"I like."

"I was hoping you'd say that. Come on, our breakfast is getting cold."

We walk hand in hand over to the table and kiss once more before sitting down.

"I can't believe this is happening," I say softly, more to myself than Gray.

"What? Is something wrong?" She is looking at me with concern.

"Everything is perfect." I reach for her hand. "I'm here with you—it's like a dream come true."

"You've dreamed of me?"

"Yes, I believe I have. I just didn't know it until that night you brought me home from the bar. You were so caring and on the edges of my drunkenness, I knew something important was happening. I didn't know what it was then." I take a deep breath. "Now that I do, I want nothing more than to explore all the possibilities with you."

"I want that too."

"Tell me, how did you know to come to the bar?"

Gray reaches for my hand. "Since that first time, I've always known where you are and what you're doing. I can't really explain it. I just knew you were in trouble that night and something led me to you."

"I'm glad. As angry as I was that you showed up, I was secretly happy, I think."

Gray laughs. "Not the vibe I got."

Although the breakfast is delicious, I don't eat much of it. My mouth is watering and it isn't because of the food. Discovering what's under Gray's robe is distracting me. I put my fork down. "Take me to bed."

Gray smiles, stands, and holds out her hand.

†

I walk with her to the bedroom, and she unties her robe. Her body is magnificent, and I can't take my eyes off it. "Guess I'm overdressed," I finally say, feeling a lump of anticipation in my throat.

Throughout the years, I haven't had many lovers. School and work occupied so much of my time that I had nothing left to invest in a relationship. If I went to bed with a woman, it was usually someone I picked up at a bar, although one was in a supermarket. Bri was the first woman I ever made love to on multiple occasions and, after our first time, our love making was mostly hot, intense, and over quickly. I don't want that with Gray.

"Let me help you with that," she says and begins to unbutton my shirt.

Suddenly, I feel shy and wonder what she is going to think when she finds I don't have a bra or panties on.

Her fingers slowly push my shirt aside.

My nipples immediately become more erect, if that is possible.

"Beautiful." As my shirt floats to the floor, her fingers gently caress my breasts before she palms my nipples.

I can feel her every touch and embrace igniting a flame that is smoldering inside me. I lean into her. "Please, Gray, make love to me."

She takes her time finishing undressing me then looks at my naked body. She lets out a long sigh before smiling. "My imagination pales in comparison to reality. You are so beautiful." Gray lets her robe fall to the floor before engulfing me in her arms. She guides me to the bed and gently lowers me before climbing next to me and cuddling.

I can feel her all around me, and I drink it all in. It is as if she is memorizing my body by touching each pleasure point. I know that behind each kiss, each caress is love incarnate. I've never known such tenderness or joy, and I drink in all that she gives me.

When her lips surround my nipple and she slowly sucks me inside her mouth, I feel my body begin to climb to new heights. I run my fingers through her hair, encouraging her for more. I am in heaven and Gray is the only one in my world. Her hand slowly makes it way down my stomach, across the mound of hair, before a finger slides the length of me. I raise my hips, encouraging her to touch me and her fingers enter me. Just when I think I am ready, her tongue is licking me while her fingers curl inside.

I am writhing as I feel my want and need climb higher, and I cry out as my body stills as the sensation of pure pleasure courses through me again and again.

Gray kisses her way up my body and smiles before tenderly kissing my lips. Our tongues entwine and, in that moment, I am lost inside everything she is. We have become one, and my heart wants nothing more than to be with her forever.

"Let me love you," I whisper into her delicious mouth. Then I begin my slow, deliberate discovery of Gray's body, leaving no part untouched. Gray responds with sighs of her pleasure, as she encourages me to linger at her breast. I can feel all the miles and years that separated us explode into a million pieces. The endless dream of Gray that I never could quite grasp is coming to fruition, and she is here with me at last.

Our hearts dissolve into one as we hold each other into the night.

†

The sound of running water wakes me from a blissful sleep. Opening my eyes, I stare at the white swirled ceiling of a suite in the Hotel Monaco in Washington DC. My body is naked, and I am sure I still feel kisses lingering everywhere as the taste and smell of Gray fills my senses. Never in my wildest imaginations could I believe anything or anyone could move me to such a passionate encounter. Yet, here I am, pulling back the soft, white sheet, letting my bare feet touch the richly carpeted floor, walking toward the bathroom, and opening the door. I can't help myself. I want—no need—to feel her luscious body next to mine again.

With a sudden trepidation that I cannot understand, I open the door. Gray turns and smiles before holding out her hand to me. I swear I can hear two voices crying "at last."

About the Author

Erin O'Reilly

Erin O'Reilly is an accomplished author with twenty-three published works, including her newest collaboration with JM Dragon *Take Me as I Am* and *Ready for Love*. She was the Sapphic Readers Award winner for her book *Deception*. Her focus as a writer is to develop strong characters that make a dramatic impact on her story lines.

When not writing, she is the Technical Director and CEO of Affinity eBook Press. Contact Erin at erinoreilly@affinityebooks.com

Other Books from Affinity eBook Press

Open Your Heart a Sensual Collection by Ali Spooner
Excite your senses, rejuvenate your memories and best of all flirt with the edge of eroticism. Allow us to help you relive that first kiss, flirting with young love, your dream come true, surprise encounters, and your wildest desires… Enjoy these stories of love, sweet seduction, and steamy encounters. Open Your Heart…a sensual collection.

Secret of Stone Creek by Natalie London
Jennifer Cameron arrives in Stone Creek, Wisconsin to sell her grandparents' large Victorian home. While there she is intrigued by a twenty-four-year-old never solved murder. Her attraction to the lovely and mysterious librarian, Diana vies for her attention. Follow this suspenseful whodunit to its conclusion.

The Promise by JM Dragon
An accidental meeting with Melissa Grant, leads to an unexpected offer for Kris Lake—refurbishing a beach cottage, with the help of Melissa's granddaughter Claire. Do outer imperfections prevent them from reaching the beauty that lives inside and the chance of a happy new life? Find out in this lovely romance that will fill you with heart-warming sensations throughout the story.

Christmas at Winterbourne by Jen Silver
The Christmas festivities for the guests booked into Winterbourne House has all the goings-on of a traditional holiday. The only difference is that this guesthouse is run by lesbians, for lesbians. Join the guests and staff at Winterbourne for a Christmas you'll not soon forget.

The Review by Annette Mori
Silver Lining, a successful lesbian romance writer, has the crazy idea to sponsor a contest where the first reader who posts a review wins a home-cooked meal with an offer to fly the winner to Washington State. Jasmine, the winner, has engaged in subtle flirtations with Silver. Bizarre messages from the unknown fan has Silver questioning the wisdom of a relationship with Jasmine.

South of Heaven by Ali Spooner
Kendra Drake has taken over as Captain of her father's shrimp boat. As a favor to her father, Kendra has agreed to give fellow shrimper, Lindsey Bowen, a chance to work on the boat but first must prove herself to Kendra and her crew. Lindsey finds a way into Kendra's heart. Will it only last for the summer?

Catch to Release by Lacey Schmidt
On the verge of success, lesbian folk-rock star, Shay Greenaura, finds herself caught up in more than just her music. Threats have her manager hiring a security firm for protection. Addison Weller, a former Diplomatic Security Services agent is called in to assess the threats against Shay. Their undeniable attraction, brewing silently between them, could prove to be a fatal distraction. Follow this fast-paced adventure to its surprising, romantic conclusion.

Ready for Love by Erin O'Reilly
Kylie Wilcox's life dramatically changed with the death of her husband. Dr. LJ Evans, a renowned archaeologist, needed and wanted nothing but her work for her happiness. Their worlds are about to collide and lives will be altered forever.

Neptune's Ring by Ali Spooner
In the sequel to *Venus Rising*, Nat and Liz, owners of Venus Rising, invite Levi and Vanessa to join them in a venture for a new club on another island. They find the perfect place in an unfinished resort, Neptune's Ring. While on the island, Levi is drawn into a mystery involving secret compartments and a murder. Join the characters in this page-turning adventure, filled with steamy romance, intrigue, and an unsolved murder.

The Ultimate Betrayal by Annette Mori
Lara is a successful, beautiful, charming, financier. She is also a total control freak, so whatever Lara wants, Lara makes sure she gets. Rachel is Lara's fun-loving, charming, irresistible wife. Sophia's surprise visit to see Lara sets in motion a number of life-changing events for them all. Hell has no fury as a woman scorned.

It's in Her Kiss by Various Affinity Authors
A collection of various holiday stories dedicated to anyone and everyone that reads it. Young, old, lesbian, gay, bisexual, and transgender. We are all the same inside and want the same things outside...love, happiness, and that special someone to spend all of our holidays with.

Keeping Faith by TJ Vertigo
You loved them in the previous novels, Private Dancer, Reece's Faith, and Reece's Star, now join the antics of Reece, Faith, Cori, Vi, and even The Animal, one last time in *Keeping Faith*.

Bound by Ali Spooner
A rogue, master vampire threatens the existence of the New Orleans vampire clan. Lord Jordan enlists Devin Benoit, sister of the Baton Rouge Alpha, and her witch lover, Tia, to assist with cleansing the city from potential disaster.

The Circle Dance by Jen Silver
Jamie Steele has moved to another town, trying to forget the heartbreak of losing her lover of six years. Sasha Fairfield finds her thoughts taken up with her ex-lover and thinks she wants Jamie back. Follow this captivating romance, as love dances through the lives of these women, to its surprising conclusion.

Search for the White Moon by Natalie London
Kathryn Austin, a government agent, is given opera singer Adriana Desi as her new assignment. Their lives and futures are in danger as the White Moon terrorists hunt them. Immerse yourself in this fast-paced, romantic thriller by debut author Natalie London.

Take Me As I Am by JM Dragon & Erin O'Reilly
When Jo Lackerly and Thea Danvers meet, an unexpected friendship develops, proving a catalyst for both women to change their lives irrevocably. Follow them on a journey of

discovery that will have your heart smiling, blood boiling, and senses entangled in a wonderful romance.

Carved in Stone by Jen Silver

Join the characters from *Starting Over* and *Arc Over Time* in this final book from the Starling Hill trilogy. Ellie Winters thinks she might be going mad when the ancient queen wants a proper burial for herself and her consort. *Carved in Stone* has romance, adventure, a treasure hunt, and happy endings for all, living and dead.

Anywhere, Everywhere by Renee MacKenzie

Gwen Martin's life in the Ten Thousand Islands area changes irrevocably when Piper Jackson comes into her life. Without trust, can the budding relationship between Gwen and Piper survive? Or will the answers to the questions continue to haunt them?

Venus Rising by Ali Spooner

Levi Johnson arrives at Venus Rising, an exclusive, lesbian-only tropical resort in the Virgin Islands, and finds more than she expected—a sizzling-hot love triangle. Torn between her attraction to both women, Levi struggles to choose the right woman to share her life.

The Devil's Tree by Ali Spooner

Torn between her love for the pack and her need to find what's missing in her life, Devin Benoit travels to New Orleans. Will the previous happenings at the Devil's Tree help or hinder Devin in the fight for her life, and the life of Tia, the woman who now owns her heart?

E-Books, Print, Free e-books

Visit our website for more publications available online.

www.affinityebooks.com

Published by Affinity E-Book Press NZ LTD
Canterbury, New Zealand

Registered Company 2517228